MOVING ON

PJ FIALA

COPYRIGHT

eBook - 978-1-942618-97-3
Paperback - 978-1-942618-54-6

Daughter of owners of Forget Me Nots, Lily - Jen Lee
Restaurant in Town, JD's Country Cooking - Jennifer Goins
Bike Shop in CO - Gil (Gilbert) Jones - Deb Jones Diem
Lake Chase and LuAnn's house is on, Waverly Lake - Ginna Honeycutt
Realtor in Durango, Leslie Peyton - Jo West
Bernstein Jewelers - Nancy Hoch
A special thank you to Marijane Diodati, my amazing editor, who despite health obstacles, came through with flying colors once again!
A special thank you to Kim Brough, for beta reading.

Last but not least, my family for the love and sacrifices they have made and continue to make to help me achieve this dream, especially my husband and best friend, Gene. Words can never express how much you mean to me.
To our veterans and current serving members of our armed forces, police and fire departments, thank you ladies and gentlemen for your hard work and sacrifices; it's with gratitude and thankfulness that I mention you in this forward.

DESCRIPTION

Let's stay in touch where bots, algorithms and subjective admins don't decide what we see. PJ Fiala's Readers' Club is my newsletter where I promise to only send you content you enjoy! https://www.subscribepage.com/pjfialafm

Series Complete!

Rolling Thunder - where bikes are built, family bonds are strengthened and love ignites.

He's living in the shadow of others,

She's newly freed from prison and learning to live again,

Together they must find their place in the world or fall apart trying.

Chase finds himself faced with straddling two worlds. He loves his job and his coworkers and he's hopeful for LuAnn's return and wants to offer her the opportunity to change her life. But considering she did time for trying to kill his boss's wife and unborn child, there's no way she'll be welcome in his professional life.

After three long years in prison, LuAnn is walking out

to a new life—with no job, no home, and no friends. Except Chase, but even then, she's treated him like shit, too, so it would be a miracle if he gave her the time of day. Somehow she has to show him she's a new woman with a clean slate—all she needs is a second chance.

How in the hell can he move them to 'Us' without losing the work family he owes his life to?

•••

Entire series complete!

USA Today bestselling author PJ Fiala brings you the full and complete Rolling Thunder series—heroes willing to sacrifice everything for the women they love. Full length novel with no cliffhanger, no cheating, and a happily-ever-after guaranteed.

LuAnn entered the room. As in, THE room. She was being processed out. Finally. Three years of her life in a 6' by 9' cell with a bunkmate. She deserved it, of course. And, in some odd way, doing time made her a changed woman. Hopefully, for the better. And, with any luck those whose lives she nearly destroyed would see it. Forgiveness? Was she asking too much? Well, that remained to be seen.

"Take a seat, LuAnn." Warden Kettleson said. LuAnn had mocked her a few times for having big ears, then felt bad about it and tried to befriend her. But Warden Kettleson didn't warm up to her. Hard to blame her.

Wearing the t-shirt and jeans that her sister had mailed to her last week so she'd have civilian clothes for today, she pulled the metal and plastic chair away from the desk and sat as quietly as she could while she waited for the Warden to look up from her paperwork.

"You have a place to stay?"

"Ye..." Her throat grated and she cleared it and started

again. "Yes. My sister, Linda, is letting me stay with her until I get on my feet."

Kettleson flipped a page in her file but never looked up. It began to make her nervous, as if she were looking for something to cancel LuAnn's release. Squeezing her hands together to stem the fidgeting that threatened to win, LuAnn sat as still as possible and focused on keeping her breathing even. Her heart beat ferociously in her chest and her skin began to sweat. Sending up a silent prayer that nothing was wrong with her paperwork, LuAnn swallowed and stared at her dreaded record Kettleson was analyzing.

"You have someone coming to pick you up?" Kettleson's voice almost sounded like a boom in the quiet room.

"Yes. A friend, Chase Matthews."

"How close of a friend is he?"

Warden Kettleson finally lifted her head and her brown eyes bore into LuAnn's blue ones.

Taking a deep breath so she didn't squirm, LuAnn answered, "He's a friend. He's the only one from my former life, besides my sister, who stayed in touch with me and visited."

"Boyfriend?"

"No."

"Hmm." Kettleson harrumphed, flipped a couple more pages, closed the book and looked directly into LuAnn's eyes.

"It looks like everything is in order." She tapped her pen on LuAnn's record, but never looked away. "I hate reoffenders, you understand? I hate releasing someone who sits here in front of me and tells me they've changed and blah blah, they're going to make it this time and on and on. So, I'm not going to ask you if you've changed. I'm not going to ask you if you've learned your lesson. But, I'm going to say this, if I ever see you back here again in this prison you will not like it. Not even a little bit. The treatment you received these past three years was only a taste of what you'll get if you come back. Plus, we'll all look upon you as if you're a two-time loser. And, don't forget it. Got it?"

Swallowing twice before responding, LuAnn nodded. "Yes."

Reaching down and laying a clear plastic bag on the desk in front of her, Warden Kettleson placed a sheet of paper alongside it.

"These are the belongings you said you wanted to keep. They've been catalogued on this sheet. Look through the bag and make sure everything listed is in there. Then sign and date at the bottom of the sheet that you've received everything."

Reaching forward LuAnn pulled the plastic bag onto her lap. She didn't want much from here. She'd been allowed three pair of shorts, three pair of underwear, three bras, three pair of sweatpants and a pair of plastic flip-flops. A comb and brush, a toothbrush, a small tube of toothpaste and deodorant. The only items that she had in her bag were a gardening book she'd been given by the librarian with permission from the warden and a separate gardening book her sister had given her on her birthday last year. It was all she had here.

Looking the meager list over, she saw the two books listed, signed her name, and added today's date - June 12. Then she closed the bag with the zip closure and waited.

Taking the sheet and sliding it in LuAnn's record, Warden Kettleson stood and held out her hand to shake, which surprised LuAnn. Nonetheless, she reached out and shook the warden's hand gripping it firmly hoping to convey a strength she didn't actually feel and almost smiled when the warden's lips almost curved into a smile. Almost.

"Remember, I never want to see you again."

"Yes, ma'am. I feel the same."

Warden Kettleson nodded at her and walked around to the front of the desk, past LuAnn and to the office door.

She opened the door and waited for LuAnn to follow her. Sliding her chair back, LuAnn gripped her plastic bag like it was her lifeline. She prayed her shaking legs would hold her up long enough to get out of this place.

Her body trembled, a mixture of fear, excitement, nerves and the unknown. The later was the most dominant feeling. What would life be like now? No more routine. No more orders.

Walking down the dingy hallway to the exit doors, she held her books close to her body. Hopefully, Chase would be waiting for her. He said he would be. But, he could have changed his mind. Dog definitely wouldn't let him off of work if he knew what he was doing.

Her mind floated to Jeremiah the last time she'd seen him. He was so angry with her. She'd done so many stupid things because of her perceived love for him. The worst of which was almost killing Joci and their unborn child. She didn't know Joci was pregnant. She also didn't think she'd take off on her bike the way she did and crash. Cutting the brake line was a fit of foolish anger and jealousy. Looking back on it now, it was hard to believe she'd stooped that low. It was the reason she'd spent the last three years in prison. None of what she didn't know was an excuse for her behavior. She'd learned that while she was here.

Shaking her head to clear thoughts of Jeremiah and all the crazy, and near fatal, things she'd done to get him to notice her, she inhaled until her lungs burned, then slowly exhaled her breath from her body.

The exit door from this unit of the prison was unlocked, the keys jingling against the metal door. She could see daylight on the other side and her heart raced. Outside for good. What a precious thought that had become. Stepping through the door she waited as it auto locked, then the warden unlocked the next door leading to the courtyard. She stepped through that door; her head automatically turning to take one last look at her garden. Two years ago, she'd been granted permission to learn to garden. She had Primrose, who was known to all as Rosie, to thank. She'd befriended Rosie, who became a mother figure to her and who loved gardening. She'd learned so much from Rosie during these past two years. She'd started to heal and found solace in the dirt, seeds, and ultimately the flowers she'd nurtured to life.

The bright hues of reds, pinks, oranges, purples and blues made her smile as Rosie was tending her gardens at this moment.

She waved at the older woman, who waved in return; they'd said their good-byes earlier today as Rosie prepared to go outside. Nodding to her friend for the last time, she turned her head toward the gate and her uncertain future. Blinking rapidly to dry the moisture that had gathered, she looked at the gate ahead that had prohibited her escape, but now allowed her passage out. She used to wonder how to escape those first few scary months when she'd cried herself silently asleep.

Not seeing a car waiting for her, she swallowed the nervousness that maybe Chase had changed his mind. Continuing to follow the warden, she told herself repeatedly, "He's here. He's here."

Warden Kettleson looked up at the guards in the tower next to the gate and nodded and a few clicks later, the gates began sliding open. They waited for the gate to close, then the outside and final gates began to slide open and her heart hammered violently in her chest. Almost there.

"Good luck to you, Mason," Warden Kettleson quietly said.

LuAnn looked up at the taller woman and nodded. "Thank you."

It was a beautiful day. The weather was a mild 78 degrees, no wind, trees and flowers were in full bloom, the grass was still a vibrant green. He'd put the top down on his Mustang convertible before he left the shop. The thrill of driving his wheels and seeing LuAnn again conflicted with Dog's look of disappointment and frustration when Chase told him why he needed the rest of the day off. Hard to blame Dog, but he'd stayed friends with LuAnn while she was incarcerated. She needed friends now more than ever before, and he was going to be that friend.

It just might mean that he would have to forego some of the shop rides in the coming days. It settled like a rock in his stomach because everyone at Rolling Thunder was and had been a family to him. He'd worked for them for close to ten years now. Dog had been the first person to help him straighten out his life when he was in his teens and he'd fucked up. He'd had to do some community service back in the day. His judgment wasn't all that good, and he'd become a real shit. Then he met JT, who shared his love of motorcycles, and who then introduced him to Dog. He hadn't really had a "home." His mother had taken off when he was a boy and his father fell into the bottle with no desire to raise Chase. His life changed when Dog took him in.

Dog demanded that he be on the straight and narrow. He had to develop manners. Take a shower every day. Be respectful. Show up to work on time, which was tough some days because he and JT used to hit the liquor pretty hard back then. But, he admired Dog and he loved JT like a brother, and he didn't want to lose them, so he straightened up. Many a night he spent at the Sheppard house. He slept on the sofa, he helped make meals. He balked the first time Dog asked him to clean the bathroom, but then he saw that JT and Ryder, JT's twin, had chores to do so he stopped gripping and did it. They'd just started Rolling Thunder and money was tight, but he always had a place to go and Dog always made sure they all ate.

Once money started rolling in, he got a raise, they all did. Then he and JT got the chance to design bikes for custom builds and his life changed forever after that. He found out that he was good at it. Really good. He had an eye for design. He had the chops to imagine what a bike would look like if he just changed this or did that. JT, too. Together, they were unstoppable.

Flipping the lever to flick on his right turn signal, he slowed and turned down the road that would lead him to the women's prison. His stomach turned over and not for the hundredth time; he wondered if he was making a mistake. Dog's face flashed before his eyes and nausea rose in his stomach. He didn't want to lose the Sheppards. He also remembered needing someone to believe in him and the Sheppards had. How could his life, which had been so bad, become so damned good and now feel as if he were throwing it away? Why the fuck couldn't life just stay good once you were lucky enough to find the good in it?

The prison came into view as he reached the crest of the hill and as it always did his stomach became queasy. By some miracle, he'd never had to go to prison. Too bad LuAnn hadn't found her salvation before she did. But thank God, she didn't kill Joci or Maddy and that she'd only been given three years. He couldn't help but worry that she still loved Dog, which is how she ended up here. Where would that leave him? Irritating Dog and the family for staying friends with LuAnn only to have her behave as she always had would end his relationship with them. He couldn't let that happen.

He pulled into the parking lot and wasn't sure what he should do from this point. Did she come out the front door or the gates? He'd been given no information on where to park or where to find her once he got here.

Twisting his wrist to see his watch, he saw that he was five minutes early and decided to get out of the car and stretch. It had been an hour's drive from home.

Opening his door, he stepped out and bent over to stretch his back. Then stood, tucked in his shirt and closed the door. Walking to the front of his car, he leaned on the hood and stared at the gates. Turning his head to the right he could see the front door, and to be honest, he still was undecided as to what to do, so he stayed where he was.

A few minutes later he heard the inner gate open and he saw her. She looked small and scared as she clutched that plastic bag in front of her. Her hair had always been dyed far too much. While she'd been in here, she'd let it grow out completely to its natural dark brown, which was far more attractive on her. The guard with her turned and said something to her and he saw her smile. That was a good sign. LuAnn nodded and the inner gate closed as the outer gate opened. LuAnn walked tentatively through the outer gate and stood in place as it closed behind her. She turned and looked at it, likely not sure what to do.

Pushing himself off the hood of his car, he began walking toward her and thought that she looked like a scared rabbit. Her fingers squeezed the contents of the plastic bag and his heart actually hurt. This was not the same woman who'd put herself in this place. He hoped that was a good thing.

She turned her head and saw him walking to her and she hesitated for a moment, then started walking to him. A few steps later, they met face to face, and she tilted her head up and smiled at him.

"Hi."

"Hi." He looked into her blue eyes, and he felt happy. "Let me carry that for you."

She looked down at the bag and clutched it tighter to her body. "Do you mind if I hang on to it? It's all I have."

His heart sank to the pit of his stomach. He reached forward and wrapped his arms around her and pulled her in for a gentle hug. "You have me." He whispered.

He heard her sob as he held her, and tears sprung to his eyes. He allowed her to cry into his chest with the stupid plastic bag between them, and he knew he'd made the right decision in coming for her today. Dog would come around. He hoped anyway.

She sniffed and pulled away, "Sorry. My emotions are all over the board today. It's surreal being out and I'm not sure what I'm supposed to do. Normally right now I'd be gardening."

He turned and wrapped his arm around her shoulders and began leading her to his car.

"Can you garden at Linda's house?"

"She said I could. My brother-in-law, Tanner, made a place in the backyard I guess."

"Well, darlin' that's a great start, don't you think?"

"Yeah."

He opened the trunk. "You want to put your bag in here, so it doesn't blow around?"

He saw her look down at her meager possessions and swallow. Good God, this just made him sad. But she carefully placed her bag in the trunk tucked safely into a corner and stepped back. He closed the lid, walked to the passenger side of his car, and opened the door for her.

"Wow, what a gentleman."

She giggled and without thinking, he said, "Dog would kick my ass if I didn't treat a woman respectfully."

She halted and looked up at him. He saw her swallow, then she slowly sat in the seat. He closed the door, chastising himself as he walked around the car for bringing up Dog so soon.

He slid into the driver's seat, put the key in the ignition and started the engine, then pulled his seatbelt over his shoulder and clicked it into place. Looking at LuAnn, he saw her put her seatbelt on. Neither of them said a word. How did you break this awkward silence?

og. The reason for her fall from grace ha, if that's what you'd call it. She never had a lot of grace. She'd been crass, nasty, bitchy and awful to everyone who mattered to her and some who liked Joci. All because she'd believed herself in love with Dog when he didn't think of her as anyone more than a little sister. He was the most handsome man she'd ever known ---tall, broad shoulders, strong, good-looking with that long, blond hair and those damned arms. Then, there was the fact that he'd made room for her at Rolling Thunder. He looked after her and Linda after their brother Lance died. She'd stupidly thought it was because he loved her, too, but that he needed time to sew his wild oats and one day, they'd be together, as in a couple.

Then Joci came along. At first, she couldn't believe that Dog seriously was interested in anyone except her. Not only was she plain, Joci was too old for Dog to be attracted to her as a girlfriend. Plus, she was Gunnar's mother for goodness sake! He was JT and Ryder's father, but he wasn't old. Joci certainly wasn't anywhere near as pretty as she was, either.

When Joci became part of Rolling Thunder, it seemed Joci was always around Dog. She was livid and green with envy. Anger hadn't begun to express her feelings; she'd felt as if Joci was stealing Dog away from her. The way he looked at Joci sent her into a rage. His treatment of Joci was like a stab in her back. Dog was hers and always would be, she fought to hold on to what she believed was the truth. Sadly, it was only her truth. And, it wasn't the truth at all. He only loved her as a kid; and she was so young she didn't understand there was a difference between loving someone as a brother or friend and being in love with them.

Taking a deep breath, she asked, "Was he mad at you?"

The tension in the car had been too much. She hated that the mood had changed.

"I suppose. He didn't say much but he gave me a look I've rarely seen from him."

LuAnn turned and looked at Chase. She saw him swallow admiring his Adam's apple as it moved up and down. There was something about an Adam's apple that had always intrigued her. It was manly and so different from a woman's throat. He had a strong jaw, a distinguished profile. He was a handsome man. A few years ago, he had a crush on her. They rode together and more than a few times they had sex. It was always great sex, too. He always made sure she was satisfied before his own pleasure came. She was so dumb to look past that. How many women would have loved to have a partner who always put her pleasure before his.

"I'm sorry." After the words were spoken, she realized that he likely thought she meant the look Dog had given him. She'd meant about all the things she'd done to Chase in her selfish quest to get Dog's attention. She'd frequently used Chase and tossed him aside at a whim.

He glanced over at her then turned his head to look at the road. "It'll be fine. He knows I've stayed in contact with you and visited you. He also knows you need a friend right now."

"Thank you for that."

Locking her fingers together in her lap, she looked out her side window at the scenery as they breezed past it all. The smells of fresh cut hay, the flowers in bloom in the gardens they passed by and the occasional dead animal swirled around her. She'd tied her hair into a ponytail at her nape this morning, but the shorter whisps of hair had fallen from the binding and now blew around her head. She held her hand over her eyes to block the sun; she didn't have a pair of sunglasses.

"If you reach in the glove box, I still have your old pair of sunglasses."

Turning her head to look at him, he had a shy grin on his face and his right shoulder hiked up then dropped.

Reaching forward she opened the glove box, and there on top of his owner's manual and insurance papers lay her sunglasses from years gone by.

Pulling them out she turned them, to and fro, examining them and trying to remember when she'd left these in his car.

"You left them in the bag of my bike. We rode during the day, but when it got dark you couldn't see through them and wore my clear goggles. I thought you might need them today."

"Thank you so much."

She put them on, the immediate difference it made in her ability to see a relief. "I owe you so much, Chase. How will I ever repay you?"

She'd been wondering this for some time, actually each time he came to visit her in prison. She assumed he'd want sex from her, right where they left off, but he hadn't made any advances toward her today. A brief hug to comfort her more than anything was all he did. Surely, a man like him would have a girlfriend by now. He was a great catch. Handsome, strong, good job, smart and easy going.

"It'll all work out, LuAnn. Right now, you need to focus on what you want to do to make money. Find a job and then make a life."

"Yeah." She swallowed and wondered for the hundredth time, how she would find a job with a prison record. People weren't always willing to give an ex-con a second chance. "So, it goes without saying that you still work full time at Rolling Thunder and we both know I'm not welcome there. So, after you drop me off at Linda's, will I see you again?"

Chase looked over at her, a sad smile on his face.

"I hope so. I thought I'd give you a few days to settle in then maybe we can go for a ride."

"I'd love that. Thank you."

They drove in silence for some time and she couldn't help thinking that this felt different. He was reserved. In the past when they'd go places or do things he'd take her hand in his. Today, his right hand was on the steering wheel, his left hand on the top of the doorframe. His hair, which was still shoulder-length, blew around as the wind swept through the car. His sunglasses hid his eyes from her, but she saw his jaw clench a time or two. He was likely just being nice. They had about fifteen minutes to go on this ride, and he'd probably not want it to be uncomfortable, so she'd follow his lead.

4

Chase watched LuAnn walk into the house with Linda and sighed heavily. Today had been harder than he thought it would be. He felt awkward and uncomfortable when he'd first seen her walking toward him. Both excited and apprehensive at what happened next, he wasn't sure if he should hug her or give her space. She seemed to understand that Dog was married, a father, happy and not at all interested in her and she seemed to be over him. But she'd been good in the past about making him believe that; and then she'd do something completely embarrassing and immature to get Dog's attention. And his heart would break a little bit more.

Backing out of Linda's driveway, he looked at the clock. He could go back to work for a while, but he didn't feel like answering any questions or hearing any snide comments. Deciding instead to go home, get his bike, and take a ride brought a smile to his face. It always did.

Making the short drive to his place, he tapped the garage door button and slowly pulled inside between his pickup and his motorcycle. He'd purchased this house two and a half years ago. It was his first big purchase. He'd gone to Dog and Joci for advice and they both came and looked at it with him. JT also popped in while they were there with the realtor and all of them had given this house the Sheppard stamp of approval. Most of the Rolling Thunder gang had helped him move in one weekend while Joci, Molly, Emma, and Kayden had helped him decorate it. Then, he'd grilled burgers and brats for everyone and had a christening party. Such good times.

Stepping into the hallway from the garage, he opened the closet door and pulled out his lightweight jacket for riding and slid it on. Walking back out to the garage, he glanced over at his sweet rides, his bike, car and truck, then did a quick perusal of his garage. He sent up a thank you to God for all he had and the friends who had helped him get there.

Staying friends with LuAnn had been the right thing to do, but it was not going to be the easiest now that she was home. More importantly, he risked losing the people who had helped him achieve all that he had. Without them, it could very well have been someone else who'd picked him up from prison today.

Hopping on his bike, his pride and joy, the bike he and JT had built from scratch at Rolling Thunder two winters ago, the heavy feeling in his heart lifted along with his hopes. Starting her up, feeling the vibration under him and hearing the low growl of the pipes made him smile. This was his happy place; riding had always been where he found his peace.

Leaving the garage, he stopped long enough to hit the garage door button from the controller in his windshield bag, then took off down the driveway and down the street heading to nowhere. The weather was still mild, the sun still high in the sky with no wind so it would be perfect to lose himself on the road for a while.

He passed Lickety Split, the little custard ice cream place about two miles from his house, and Olivia waved to him from the big service window.

Thoughts of her raced through his head. Over the past couple of years that he lived in this area of Green Bay, he had stopped in there. Olivia had given him every indication that she was available and interested. At one point, Olivia had asked him, "Are you ever going to ask me out?" To which he replied, "If I answer that, I'll ruin the surprise."

A week later he stopped in and asked her out, but she had a date that night and he never asked her again. She'd told him just a couple of months ago that she was no longer seeing that man and he took the hint. But by that time, he knew LuAnn was going to be getting out and he didn't want to get involved. First, because he had every intention of remaining friends with LuAnn. Secondly, women never appreciated or tolerated a man remaining friends with his exes, and LuAnn was an ex. They'd spent many nights together with little sleep.

Now though, he wasn't sure where he and LuAnn were going. If he compared the two women, it seemed like a no-brainer that Liv was likely the better choice for him. She owned Lickety Split, built it from the ground up, managed it and did a bang-up business. Liv was beautiful with her long, blond hair and big blue eyes, full lips and a sexy body. She was the total damned package.

LuAnn by comparison used to have blond hair. She had a stellar body and he remembered how she felt pulled tightly against him. How she felt when he made love to her. All of it. It was what a man fantasized about when he dreamed of a woman to spend his life with. Her lips knew just how to fit perfectly to his. Her mouth, when she sucked his cock, fuck, she swirled her tongue at just the perfect time then sucked down hard on him and his engines revved at full speed. But, and it was a big but, she wasn't in love with him; she loved Dog. And, that was the part that hurt the most.

Riding down the country road that led him away from home, he enjoyed the horses running and playing in the pasture as he past the Olson farm. Turning right at the first road, he sped down the straight road to clear the negative thoughts out of his head, then made the next right and headed toward home.

As he entered the town line, he found himself in front of Lickety Split. Without another thought, he pulled in to get himself a custard cone and chat with Liv.

5

Dragging the bag of weeds toward the garage, LuAnn enjoyed the freedom of being able to leave the area without asking permission. She'd spent this past week creating Linda and Tanner's flower beds. Her sister wasn't shy about the fact that she knew nothing about gardening and what's more, she really didn't want to learn. LuAnn found herself feeling useful in beautifying their home and reflecting on what came next.

Tanner made it perfectly clear that he was less than happy she was staying in their home. He and Dog got along great, of course, and LuAnn was a source of embarrassment to him. Dinners were quiet, and she'd fought the urge to eat in her room for a couple of reasons. First, she needed to be sure she didn't shut herself away. Secondly, she deserved his annoyance. She thought that if she desensitized herself to his treatment, it wouldn't hurt so bad when she finally gathered her nerve to leave the house. She would be less scared when she left their home, too.

"How's it coming?"

LuAnn jumped at Linda's voice as she entered the garage.

"Good. Come out and take a look; I think you'll be happy."

She deposited the bag of weeds alongside the garbage can to toss later and exited the garage with her sister behind her.

"I have day lilies scattered throughout the garden in various colors. Each corner has the wheat grass that I moved from that back corner, which adds height and movement. The dragon lilies and the dusty tall sedum are over there, and I'll be adding some coral bells after I go to the greenhouse."

"Oh, my goodness, LuAnn, look how pretty everything is. And, you've done all of this without buying anything."

"You had it all here, Linda, we just needed to find it among the weeds." She looked proudly over what she had accomplished and couldn't wait to see it all in a few weeks when everything fully bloomed.

Linda pulled her into a huge hug and LuAnn hugged her back. It brought tears to her eyes to have someone hold her and genuinely be happy. It had been so long. Even when Chase had first dropped her off a week ago, Linda politely hugged her. While she appreciated the feeling, she could tell it was because Linda felt like it was what she was supposed to do.

Sniffing, Linda pulled back and looked at her. They both had blue eyes; their brother, Lance, also had had the same blue eyes. God, she missed him. He'd been dead about nineteen years now and not a day went by that she didn't think of him especially while she'd been in prison. She was guilty of committing crimes that had landed her in prison and knew Lance would be so ashamed of her. He loved Dog so much.

"Are you crying?"

"No." She swiped quickly at her eyes and looked away from Linda.

"You are to crying. Why on earth are you sad?"

Shaking her head, she sniffed. "I'm not sad. It felt good for you to hug me. I haven't had a genuine honest to goodness hug in years."

Linda pulled her in for a hug again, this time it was slower, but firm, and completely from the heart.

"I love you so much, Lu. I guess things have been a bit stressed recently. I'm so sorry if I've made you feel like you aren't welcome. It certainly wasn't my intent. I'm so happy to have you back. I just wanted to give you time to adjust. Sadly, I didn't realize how in doing so I made you feel unwanted."

That didn't help her to stop crying, it actually made it a bit worse, and she sobbed in Linda's arms. Her body shook as her sister held her close and whispered sweet words in her ear.

"It's all going to be alright, Lu. From here on out, you've got your head on straight and you're going to be successful at anything you want to do."

Squeezing Linda as hard as she could, she mumbled into her shoulder, "I hope so."

"You will. You're smart. You're talented. Look at my yard. Maybe you should be working in a greenhouse."

She giggled then. "Great minds. I was just thinking that today. When I get plants tomorrow, I thought I'd see if they have any job openings. My only problem is I don't have a phone. You don't have a landline. What number will I give them on my application?"

"Tanner and I just talked about this last night. I thought we could go this afternoon and get you a phone. I'll pay for it until you get a job, then you can take it over, deal?"

Pulling back, she looked into her sister's eyes. "I promise you I will get a job somehow and I'll pay you back."

Linda's hands came up and framed her face, her thumbs swiped at the tears that tracked down LuAnn's cheeks and she smiled, "I know you will, honey. I know you will."

Linda stepped back and moved to admire her yard once more. The smile on her face was all LuAnn needed to know that she loved what she saw. Linda turned and looked at her, the smile on her face grew.

"Let's go clean up then get you a phone."

Giggling LuAnn nodded, "Sounds good."

Going back into the garage, she dumped the weeds into the garbage can, dusted her hands off and walked into the house with Linda right behind her.

She walked into the kitchen, turned left and then left again and went downstairs to the basement, which was now her bedroom. She had a bathroom there as well. The temperature stayed cool and Linda had kept all of her old clothes hanging neatly in the closet in her bedroom for her return to society. Looking through her clothes again today, just as she had these past few days, she shook her head. She'd dressed like a whore. All of the shirts and t-shirts were low-cut, exposing half her breasts. She'd always been well-endowed, but now she looked at herself with new eyes.

Linda had kept all the pictures she'd had before prison and the bleached-out hair, dark makeup, and tight pants, were, God, how embarrassing. How did she not see it before? What on earth, besides the fact that she was an easy lay, did Chase ever see in her?

She pulled out a pair of jeans, and since she'd lost a fair amount of weight in prison, they no longer looked like a streetwalker's pants. They actually had a little looseness to them, which suited her just fine.

The past couple of nights she'd taken a couple of her lowest cut t-shirts and sewed material from another shirt that matched to cover up her cleavage. Selecting the dark-blue t-shirt she'd modified last night and a pair of jeans, she headed into her bathroom to clean up and begin to integrate into society.

6

Turning his motorcycle into the driveway, the first thing Chase noticed was the flower beds. They were pristine, clean, and vibrant. Clearly LuAnn had been busy these past couple of weeks.

Dropping the kickstand, he dismounted and walked to the front door. Before he neared it, the door opened, and LuAnn stepped outside. Her smile was tentative, almost shy, but beautiful to see.

She flipped her dark hair over her shoulder, "Hi."

"Hi. It looks like you've been busy."

Her head turned toward the flower bed along the front of the house and her smile grew more becoming than before.

"Yeah, it's been fun watching it transform. I have pictures, too."

Reaching into the front pocket of her denim shorts, she pulled out a phone and tapped a few times. Stepping from the top step, she met him halfway up the sidewalk and showed him a picture.

"You can scroll through if you like there aren't many."

"When did you get a phone?"

"Oh, about four days ago. Linda took me to get it."

"You didn't call to tell me you had one." The disappointment he felt was like a punch in the gut.

"Chase, I don't want to put pressure on you." She tucked her hair behind her ear, and he noticed her hand shaking.

"Hey," he waited for her to look up at him. "No pressure, okay? I want to stay in touch with you, LuAnn. I want to..." What? What did he want? He wanted her. All of her. But, when he thought about going back to where they'd been his stomach tightened up and his heart felt heavy.

She quietly waited for him to say more but he couldn't articulate what he wanted to say. So, he pulled up her contacts in her phone, added his phone number, sent himself a text so he had her number and handed it back to her.

"Now you have my number in your phone and I have yours."

She smiled at him and swallowed as she took her phone back.

"I got a job." Her cheeks turned pink as if she was embarrassed to say it.

"That's fantastic, where?"

"The greenhouse on County E, Forget Me Nots. I'm only working in the back, tending to the plants and flowers, but it's perfect. I started two days ago. They know all about my past and my record, but they were willing to give me a chance. The couple that owns it are both from Germany and speak very broken English, so communication has been interesting. But, I just go in and work hard and so far they've been pleased with me. Jan, one of the owners, has taken to just giving me a thumbs-up when I do good. It works."

"I'm proud of you, LuAnn. You're really going to do well."

She nodded, opened her mouth to say something, but choked up and looked over at the flowers. "Would you like to come in and see the arrangement of flowers I did for Linda with some extras from the greenhouse? They turned out so pretty."

"Sure."

He followed her into the house. No lights were on, but the large picture window allowed the sunlight from outside to fill the room and it looked bright and cheery. A fireplace on the far wall was framed in light brown brick; on the hearth sat a full arrangement of flowers in oranges, reds and yellows. It was bright and happy.

"I made this one."

"I don't know much about flowers, LuAnn, but this is fantastic. Very bright."

She walked over to the arrangement and picked a dead leaf from one of the flower stems, then turned to him; her smile said it all, she was proud of herself, too. It was becoming on her. This new demeanor and the lack of crassness she'd had before was gone and replaced with a shyness and simplicity that was hard to resist.

"Thank you. Did you want something to drink?"

He shook his head slightly. "I actually stopped by to see if you wanted to go for a little ride."

Her smile. Wow. He felt sucker punched. Her blue eyes lit with excitement as she clapped her hands in front of her.

"Really? Oh, yes, I'd love that. I've missed it so much. I just need to run down and change into a pair of jeans if you don't mind. I'll be fast, I promise."

He chuckled. "Go ahead, I can wait."

She skipped from the living room and he heard her

saying something to someone in the kitchen. Stepping into the dining room, which faced into the kitchen, he saw Linda wiping down the counters. Linda and LuAnn looked similar, though Linda was about four years older. She remained trim and her dark brown hair was a bit shorter than LuAnn's.

"Hi, Chase, come on in. I understand you two are going for a motorcycle ride."

"Yeah, it's a perfect night for it. The temperature is supposed to drop below 85 in an hour or so, which will make it even better."

"It sounds lovely. I know LuAnn is very excited to go. I watch her working on the landscaping and every time she hears a motorcycle, she turns her head to see if she can see it. I'm going to take a guess and say she's been watching for you."

Linda smiled and guilt flooded his chest.

"I wanted to give her some time to settle in."

Moving another flower arrangement from the corner of the counter, she pointed to it. "LuAnn brought this one home today and I just over watered it; you caught me cleaning up my mess."

"She sure does like her flowers."

He admired the colorful array from his standpoint. He knew next to nothing about flowers except that women liked roses and he could probably pick a rose out of a group of flowers if he had to. Other than that, all he knew was that they were colorful, the colors all seemed to go together and this one was different than the one in the living room.

"She's going to have our house filled with them before long. She tells me not to worry, she won't go overboard." Linda laughed but looked lovingly at the flowers before adding, "she's doing pretty good, Chase. She's changed for sure and she feels so bad about what she's done."

Nodding he looked Linda in the eyes. "Yeah, I know."

"How are you doing?"

The question surprised him. He didn't have an answer though. How was he doing? He'd tested himself by stopping in at the Lickety Split a few nights ago and Liv made time to chat with him. It was such a puzzle to him that as attractive, smart and self-reliant as she was, he couldn't take the next step with her. He almost asked her out, but guilt washed over him about LuAnn and he just couldn't do it. He'd spent the rest of these past few days trying to figure it out. Then he finally decided to take LuAnn for a ride to see if guilt washed over him in the same way.

LuAnn came running up the stairs from the basement in a nice fitting pair of jeans, a pair of black boots and a nice tank top that fit higher than her older clothing had. She was slimmer than she used to be, but her curves, man oh man, she had the perfect curves. His heartbeat accelerated at the reminder of how she felt against his body.

"You look fantastic, LuAnn."

She smiled brightly, gave the top of her tank top a bit of a tug up to make sure she was covered and softly said, "Thank you. I've lost weight while I was...recently."

7

Climbing on the back of Chase's bike was a little bit like going back in time except that he had a different bike now. New. Sleek. Sexy design that he said he and JT built a couple of winters ago. He'd mentioned it at one of his visits to the prison, but she'd never actually seen it.

"Your bike is stunning. You did a fantastic job."

He turned his head and she instinctively leaned over that shoulder to hear him. "Thanks. I'm proud as hell of it."

Her heartbeat sped up and his cologne wafted to her nose. He smelled so good like fresh cool sage and citrus. Closing her eyes, she remembered the last time they'd had sex. They'd ridden all day up to Door County along the shoreline. Stopped and had lunch at an outside bistro, then on the way home they'd taken the backroads all along the bay and marveled at the outrageously expensive homes along the water. The sun was beginning to set and the whole day outside with him had been fantastic. Arriving back at his apartment, he offered her a beer, then another. They'd sat on his tiny deck off the living room and watched the neighbors argue about something then they'd gone inside. As soon as the door was closed, he grabbed her from behind and pulled her tightly to his body. His strong arms wrapped around her waist and his cock thickened against her backside. It didn't take long after that and they were naked and stumbling to his bedroom. She remembered it so well. She'd thought about it so many times at night while she was in prison. The second he entered her; her body came alive. They fit together so well, and he loved lavishing attention on her breasts. He'd pumped into her a few times then stop to pull a nipple into his mouth, pump a few more times then give the other nipple equal attention. The sensations drove her wild along with the weight of his body on hers. Two days later, she was on the run hiding from the cops and the following day she was arrested. She'd been so incredibly foolish. Her mind wasn't on Dog when Chase was on her, why hadn't that thought struck her until now? She'd been blinded by what she'd thought she wanted; she'd been so certain of her womanly feelings, she ended up acting like a child. Now she was an ex-con.

Chase backed them out of Linda's driveway, started his bike, then off they went. He turned left at the stop sign at the end of the street and she immediately knew where they were going. Just like in years past, they'd drive along the edge of town, along the farms and enjoy life outside of the city, not that Green Bay was all that big, but the farms were so pretty. They were alive with plants and animals and machinery doing any number of things.

Wrapping her arms tighter around his waist and resting her chin on his right shoulder she looked ahead to the little brick church on the edge of the county. She'd always adored it and sometimes he'd pull in. They'd sit and admire the ancient stonework and chat.

The bike slowed and a smile formed on her lips as he down shifted twice before applying the brakes, then turned right into the church parking lot. Riding to the back of the lot, he turned the bike, so it was facing the road, then shut it off, dropped the kickstand and waited for her to get off.

Reluctantly she removed her arms from around his waist and dismounted. Walking a few steps toward the old church she marveled at the fact that everything looked exactly the same outside.

"It's beautiful. I thought of this place so many times over the past few years."

"It is. I've become a member of it since you've been gone. I like the Pastor, Greg. He's not much older than I am." He moved closer to her and she looked up into his eyes, a stunning smile on his face. "And, he rides."

"No way!"

His smile grew and it was mesmerizing. How had she never admired this about him before? "Yep. After church on Sundays, we usually go for a little ride and have lunch. He's brought me so much peace."

Tears sprung to her eyes at Chase needing to find peace. Had she hurt him so bad? And again, how could she never have known this? She'd been such a selfish person; she'd never seen anyone else's pain but her own. Wrapping her right arm around his waist, she squeezed him, and relief surrounded her when he wrapped his left arm around her shoulders.

"I'm sorry you needed to find peace, but I'm grateful Greg was here for you."

Chase inhaled deeply and slowly let his breath leave his body.

"I honestly didn't know I needed to find peace, either, LuAnn. But, I was out of sorts when you went to prison. My thoughts and feelings were all over the place--- anger, jealously, revenge, even a bit of hatred. I started to act recklessly again. Driving too fast, snapping at my friends for no reason. Then, just like it was meant to be, Greg brought his bike into Rolling Thunder and I happened to be working. He was looking for a longer kickstand for his bike, and he wanted a backrest, so I started helping him. We talked long after the shop closed. He told me he was the Pastor of Grace Church. I couldn't believe it. I told him we'd sat outside of the church a number of times because it was so beautiful. He invited me to service on the following Sunday. Then he said maybe we could go for a ride afterward. So, I did. A couple of years later I asked him if he offered to go for the ride, so I'd come to church and all he did was wink at me."

Closing her eyes, she wrestled with all of this information. Stepping away from Chase she walked over to the little bench at the side of the building and sat down. She tried holding back the tears that stung her eyes. What in the hell had she done? And why? For what? Look what she'd done to Chase and Dog and Joci. Shit, she hadn't even begun to let herself think of all she'd put them through.

Staring out across the small cemetery that lay alongside the church, she fought hard not to think about the sadness and heartache she'd been responsible for. Swiping at her cheeks, she felt the wetness of her tears without realizing she was crying. She didn't deserve to be here. She didn't. Guilt and suffering were heavy on her shoulders and she felt as though she'd crumble from their weight.

The soft sound of shoes on pavement brought her back to consciousness and she heard Chase's voice.

"Hey there, I'd like to introduce you to LuAnn."

"I'd be honored," said a second voice.

Swiping feverishly at her face, horrified that she looked

a fright, she then wiped her wet fingers on her pant leg and blinked rapidly to clear her vision.

A nice-looking man in his thirties came to stand before her. He wore blue jeans and a Harley shirt with flames in blue on the bottom of the hem and the sleeves. His blond hair and green eyes were friendly, his smile exceedingly kind.

He held his hand out to her, "Hello, LuAnn, I'm Greg, Chase's friend."

She stood and took his hand in hers. "Hi, it's so nice to meet you but how do you know who I am?"

"Call it a lucky guess. Chase wondered if you'd need another friend and thought I might fit the bill. Anytime you want to talk, I'm here."

She looked up at the sky, certain there would be a lightning bolt shooting down to smite her. She was ready. Or was she?

Staring at the ceiling, Chase's heart felt a bit lighter. He felt sort of bad ambushing LuAnn with Greg, but Greg had told him that if he and LuAnn were to ever have a chance at any kind of relationship, she had to come to terms with what she'd done. Not that she didn't know what she'd done, clearly she did, but she had no idea what her actions had truly done to the people around her. She had to confront the aftermath of what she'd done. She either had to accept it, deal with it, and make amends with those she'd wronged, or she'd just continue to do rash things without thought as to the consequences of them.

She'd cried so much tonight. She'd made an appointment to talk with Greg tomorrow after work. When he'd dropped her off tonight at Linda's, he'd softly kissed her lips and said, "Call me when you want to see me again, Lu."

He'd hopped on his bike without another word and left her standing on the front stoop. Now he lay here wondering if he'd done the right thing. But, they had to start somewhere; avoiding the people she'd hurt wasn't the answer and Greg would help her see that. Sunday he'd walk into church, pray for guidance, maybe ride with Greg and come home as usual. By then, he'd know if LuAnn ever wanted to see him again. She had about four days to think about it.

Rolling onto his side, he scrunched his pillow under his head, pulled his phone off the nightstand and tapped on his photo's icon. Scrolling through the pictures, he looked at the pictures he had of LuAnn from years ago. She was unrecognizable in them. Still the same great tits and ass, but even the look on her face was one of unhappiness. She didn't have any peace in her heart back then, either, it was easy to see now. A couple of pictures of them together showed they were both in that same place, but he'd had the guidance of Dog and the Rolling Thunder crew, she didn't.

His phone rang, he looked at the time first, just after ten, then looked at the caller - JT.

"Hey man, what's up?"

"Chase, I just called to tell you I'm a married man."

"What? I thought you were getting married with Ryder and Gunnar. A threesome or something."

JT chuckled. "Man, I just couldn't take all that wedding shit. Kayden and I are so fucking busy with our jobs and Kayden hasn't been feeling well lately. I said, 'Let's just go and get married, the three of us.' And she damned near cried she was so relieved. So, we got married this after-noon at the church with no one there but us, the Pastor and two office gals as witnesses."

Chase sat up. Pride for his friend being his true self and happiness for him flooded through him. "Wow, good for you, man and congratulations to you, Kayden and Dakota. I hope Kayden feels better soon."

JT's laugh sounded over the phone. "She will in about seven months."

It took a moment to sink in what he was saying, then he laughed along with his friend. "Holy fuck, you're going to be a dad?"

"Well, I'm already Dakota's dad, but yeah, Kayden's baking me a bun."

The laughter flew freely from him. His joy for the one constant in his life all these years real. "Good for you, JT. Man, I'm sorry I wasn't there to witness it, but I hope you'll at least toss a little shindig and celebrate."

"For sure we will. We're going to wait until after the big double shindig. Then, we'll do something smaller. Also, we didn't invite anyone to be there so no one would have hard feelings."

"It makes perfect sense. I'm truly happy for you, bud."

JT laughed again. "Gotta go and get jiggy with my woman, you know, sealing the deal for sure. Talk to you later, bro."

The line went dead before he could say anything more and his cheeks actually hurt from smiling so broadly for his friend. JT had always been his own man. When he met Kayden out in Sturgis, she fit him so well it was uncanny. She didn't get all involved with the girly stuff; she didn't care if she was part of a group or off doing her own thing. It was a thing of beauty watching those two, well, three with Dakota, meld into a family. It also made him a little sad; it was the one thing he didn't have in his life and he realized right now, he wanted it.

Plugging his phone in for the night, he set it back on the night table, rolled onto his back and stared again at the ceiling. Life was hard. How he would manage it next remained to be seen.

9

Scrolling through her pictures, LuAnn's smile couldn't be wiped off her face. The flowers she'd tended were a thing of beauty, God's beauty, she was just the caretaker. She and Chase had a beautiful ride this evening and tomorrow she'd meet with Greg and begin another healing session. It was different from finding the gardening and flowers as a form of peace. This peace, as Greg said, would come from within.

As kids, she, Linda and Lance never attended church or belonged to one. Chase said he'd found peace in God and the community of church, which had been helpful, since his Rolling Thunder family had distanced themselves in a way. He told her that they knew he had stayed in contact with her, was visiting her in prison, and naturally, they felt betrayed by that and maybe mad at him. At least that was Chase's feeling. An invisible wall, especially each day after he'd gone to visit her. But, his friends at Rolling Thunder, JT, Ryder and Gunnar especially, were also moving on with their own lives and with that came less time for him.

Dog had said he understood when Chase explained

why he wanted to remain in contact with her. But, Dog was fierce in his protectiveness and his love of his family, and he loved Joci and their children. LuAnn had tried to harm Joci and Maddy.

Inhaling deeply and letting it out in a whoosh, she hoped Greg could help her get over this sick feeling in her stomach every time she thought about the Sheppard family.

She scrolled to a picture she'd taken this evening of Chase and Greg talking, both of them smiling, and she stared at it. Chase had thought enough of her to introduce her to one of his friends. He was a good person and he genuinely wanted to help her and that was heartwarming. But the doubts that ran through her head were whether she was a project to him. A way of paying it forward, so to speak. And, if she managed to get herself together, would he then move on? That, right now, sent fear running through her body.

Closing her photo app, then setting her phone on the bedside table, she rolled to her side and looked at the night sky from the window in her bedroom. The stars twinkled in the midnight sky, some of them brighter and more prominent, some of them were distant, less obvious and cast a fainter glow. She used to feel as if you weren't the center of attention, the brightest star, you didn't exist. Now, more than anything, she wanted to be a distant star, happy to be lighting the sky in a less obvious way.

***

Digging in the fresh soil she'd mixed with nutrients and vitamins; LuAnn enjoyed the feel of the cool dirt between her fingers and the fresh, clean, scent that wafted to her nose. Hearing a clatter, she looked up to see Joseph, a fellow worker, pick up the shovel he'd dropped; his cheeks were bright red from the sun he'd been out in all morning and probably because he'd just created a loud noise in the otherwise quiet of the greenhouse. Other than fans blowing in the background, the solitude of working back here was comforting.

Joseph walked toward her, slowly, as was his usual, and nodded.

In his slow southern drawl, he said, "Morning, Ms. LuAnn."

"Morning, Joseph. Looks like you've gotten some sun this morning already."

"Yes, Ma'am. It's gonna be a scorcher today. Already 86 out."

Glancing out the greenhouse windows to the bright sky she nodded. "Yeah, but I just love this weather."

Joseph chuckled, his yellowed teeth always making her feel grateful for her own good dental hygiene. "Gotta say, I do, too. I'm still not used to these Wisconsin winters."

Standing and relaxing her back from the bent position she'd been in, she smiled at him. "I detect a southern accent, so let me guess. Maybe, Tennessee."

Joseph chuckled. "Close, Kentucky."

Nodding she continued. "What brought you here to this very different climate than Kentucky?"

His cheeks deepened in color as he sheepishly replied, "I was in prison for fifteen years, Ms. LuAnn. After I got out and went home, I quickly realized I wasn't welcome there. So, I threw a dart at a map and I ended up here."

Swallowing the fear in her throat, she asked, "What gave you the impression you weren't welcome at home?"

She dreaded hearing the answer; her stomach tightened just waiting for his response in case it was what she feared the most.

"All my old friends had moved on, didn't want me around 'cause I was trouble. Had a hard time finding work.

The place I was living in was only a half-way house and I had to move on in six months and hanging around with other half-ways didn't exactly set me on the right path. Many of them were getting in trouble while supposedly straightening themselves out. My social worker told me to move on, get a job and keep my nose clean."

"So, they let you leave the state, but don't you have to report to a Parole Officer?"

"Yes, ma'am. They transferred me to a PO here in Green Bay once I told them where I wanted to go."

She nodded and smiled at him. "Looks like it's working out for you, Joseph."

"Yes, ma'am. If it weren't for Jan and John's willingness to hire ex-cons, I'd likely still be looking."

Sadness settled in her heart. That would likely be her life moving forward.

"Yes, they seem like good people."

"Yes, ma'am. I better be gettin' on. Talk to you later, Ms. LuAnn."

"Talk to you later, Joseph."

She watched him walk a few slow steps, then continued working the nutrients and vitamins into the soil. She'd be replanting Zinnia's today, one of her favorites.

10

"Chase, will you be around this year to help with the Veteran's Ride?"

Chase stood from his bent position cutting a piece of metal to fabricate part of a gas tank on a new bike design he had come up with. JT was off the remainder of this week and next, spending time with his new wife, enjoying some honeymoon time. So, he had the chance to create something truly his own. Looking at Dog, his boss, mentor and father figure, he nodded.

"Of course, nothing's changed this year."

Dog stepped closer; his long blond hair pulled back into a ponytail at the nape of his neck. His tattooed arms, still beefy and strong at his age crossed in front of him as Dog stared at him.

"Chase, I know you're straddling a thin line, but LuAnn can't be here. As you can imagine, none of us want to see her. I understand if that makes it especially hard for you and I'm sorry for that. I also don't want you to have to keep making choices between us and her, but it's just too soon."

Swallowing hard Chase looked into Dog's eyes. He saw honesty and earnestness and also...fear.

"I know, Dog. I'll tell her tonight that I won't be around much while we're pulling this together. Believe it or not, she feels such remorse and regret over what she's done. She'll also understand."

Dog nodded, uncrossed his arms and held his right hand out. Taking Dog's hand in his, they shook hands, a firm grip as he was taught, and Dog's lips turned up in a faint smile.

"Thanks, Bud."

Dog then pulled him forward and wrapped his left arm around Chase's shoulders and hugged him. Stepping away Dog nodded and turned to walk across the design shop floor to the door leading out to the garage area. The heaviness in his heart lightened a bit after Dog hugged him, but it was still there. LuAnn better not screw this up and cause him to lose this whole family. Although, he was likely to lose them anyway, sooner rather than later, if things kept up like this. How long could you lead a double life before it caught up to you?

Needing to beat on something to relieve some of the pressure building in his chest, Chase grabbed a rubber mallet and the piece of metal he'd just cut. He walked to the shaping wheel to beat this piece of metal into a rounder version of what it was right now.

Whacking the hammer against the metal over and over not only brought a searing pain up his arm to his shoulder, but his body broke out into a sweat, which not only trickled down his temples and onto his shirt, but ran down the middle of his back, drenching his shirt. If only life were as easy to mold as metal, things could be better. Watching the flat nondescript metal begin forming into the side of a gas tank, he marveled at the changing shape of it. The fact that he was causing it to change shape had him musing that this was his life right now. He could beat the shit out of it and make it what he wanted, or he could lay there like a flat piece of metal and not do anything and let someone else beat his life into something unrecognizable. But now in his late twenties, wasn't it time to make more of himself? The adolescent that Dog had largely taken in and shaped by sometimes beating the crap out of him and molding him into a respectable human, now was making a nice income, had learned a trade from Dog, paid his bills, and then bought his first house something ten years ago seemed like a total impossibility for him to achieve, especially on his own; he had been shaped like this metal. He was a rounder, softer version of the kid he'd been, was he finished being shaped and molded or did he have more change coming? Two more whacks with the hammer told him; he was still being molded and shaped, only now, he needed to be the one wielding the hammer.

Finishing this section of the tank, he heard the doors opening and closing and knew it was quitting time. Checking the clock on the far wall, just under the Rolling Thunder logo, he saw the hands on the clock confirming it was quitting time. Wiping his hands on the closet shop rag, he organized his tools, put them back in his toolbox another large purchase he'd made on his own, and locked it up for the night.

Proud of his cleaned-up work area, he grabbed his lunch box and headed to the time clock to punch out.

Securing his empty lunch box onto the bag on the back of his bike, Chase threw his leg over the seat, looked up into the bright sunlit sky and tried to mentally rehearse telling LuAnn he'd not be around as much as he'd like in the coming couple of weeks. The look on her face would likely say it all, but she had to know this was coming. It was a Rolling Thunder tradition.

Starting his bike up, he revved the engine a couple of times, never tiring of the growl of the pipes and the low throaty hum the motor made. Damn he loved this bike. He'd done a fantastic job with it, too. The compliments abounded every time he took her out and it confirmed his belief that he was good at designing and building. JT got most of the credit at the shop for the designs and with his partnership with Blaze Tires, that recognition only grew. But, it rankled a little bit that he never got any credit for all of the time and effort he put into each design. No, lately it was beginning to rankle a lot if he were honest.

Shaking the gloom from his mind, he heeled the kickstand up, stepped on the shift lever to drop it down into first gear and took off out of the parking lot and headed toward home.

The warm summer air dried the sweat from his skin and cooled it as he maneuvered his baby up onto the highway for the fifteen-minute ride home. Traffic was still light but would soon congest this stretch of the highway as all day workers headed toward home. That's why he liked leaving work on time, he could get on and then off the highway before it filled with terrible drivers angry from their shitty days at work with people they didn't like and over-bearing bosses. He didn't have that. He loved his co-workers. And his boss, even though they were at odds at the moment. It would get better though, he had faith and Greg had told him to stay the course, pray for guidance but to stay true to himself. That was his plan, but how hard would it get?

11

*L*uAnn sat at the table of The Grill, a cute hometown type restaurant that was owned by one of Greg's parishioners. He'd suggested the place to her, and she was eager to see it after hearing him talk about the good food.

The door opened and a bell hanging on the arm of the door rang out alerting staff, and customers, of the arrival or the exit of a customer. This time it was the latter, and she sank back, almost sad it wasn't Greg.

The waitress, a nice elderly lady with pure white hair, cut short and curled at the ends, making it look fuller than it was, stopped by her table. According to her badge, her name was Judy, and her pink lipstick had begun to fade as her day had worn on.

"Here's your iced tea, Hon. Anything else I can get you?"

LuAnn smiled at her, "No, thank you. I'm waiting for someone, but he may want something once he arrives."

"Sure thing, Doll, I'll be sure to stop back."

The bell rang, and the door opened again. She was relieved to see Greg, looking freshly showered, walk toward her table. Judy stopped and Greg pointed to her, then Judy scurried off. Greg sat across from her, reached out his hand and shook hers, then started right in.

"I'm sorry I'm a little late, I had a bit of an emergency this afternoon and had to be out at a parishioner's farm, which then required a shower on my part."

"Oh, I hope everything will be alright."

He smiled and she marveled at his handsome features. Not as tall as Chase, he was likely around 5'10", blond hair, cut short and business-like, green, sparkling eyes and the faintest hint of a dimple in his right cheek. She hadn't noticed that when she'd met him yesterday.

"It'll all be fine. They have strong faith and good hearts; they'll be just fine. Plus, the church family is very good at helping each other out, so they have a huge support network."

She smiled. What on earth was that like? Having a huge support network. After her brother, Lance, died, she'd never really had a support network besides Linda. In the early days after Lance passed away, she had Dog helping them out, but she could see now it was more out of duty than love or friendship and he had his own kids to support and look after not to mention being a father figure to Chase. She'd been more of a burden than anything. If only she'd had realized it sooner.

"That's good to hear."

"So, LuAnn, I wanted to see you here today because I thought it might be good to have our first meeting outside of my office. I know that it's very slow at this time of day and we aren't near anyone. I don't expect that it will break penitent-clergy privilege since no one is anywhere near our table and I know that you've been in prison, but it's up to you. The privilege is yours, not mine.

"I'm fine with it, Greg. It's actually more relaxing."

"Good. I know from Chase what you did and that you want to find peace by confronting it and hopefully making amends. But, I don't know what kind of support you have or, for that matter, what sort of faith you have, if any. So, as a start, if I can answer any spiritual questions for you, I'd love to do so. If you decide you'd like us to meet so that you can find the peace you want and deserve, I'd be happy to counsel you. Think of me as your spiritual guide. We'd focus on what happened three years ago, how to seek amends, and then move on to how to direct your life going forward. I'm happy to be of assistance to you."

The heat climbed up her chest, then her throat and into her cheeks as the embarrassment enveloped her.

"I'm afraid I'm not all that spiritual. We never really went to church; I've never belonged to one and I have to say I don't know where to begin."

"Well, let's begin like this. What or who do you think of when I say God?"

Biting her lower lip, she watched a bead of moisture roll down the side of her iced tea glass and then another. The rivulets of droplets began sliding down, wetting the napkin her glass sat on and the wet ring around the glass grew larger.

"I don't really know. I guess I think of Him as an all-powerful and all-knowing being."

"That's a great start." He looked up when Judy brought him a glass of soda and set it down in front of them.

"You all want something to eat this afternoon?"

Greg looked at her, a smile on his face. "The pie here is to die for."

Just then her stomach growled, and she laughed.

"I suppose I could try a piece of pie."

"Perfect. May I order for us?" Greg's eyes danced with glee as he waited for her response.

"Sure."

He turned his smile to Judy and ordered. "Judy, we'd each like a piece of your apple caramel sea salt pie, please."

Judy's smile made her look ten years younger. "Oh, thank you, Pastor. Coming right up."

He looked back at her and winked. "Judy is the master behind the pies and she just loves it when people eat and rave about them."

Giggling she thought, as always, he was likely the nicest man she'd ever met.

"Now, let me tell you about my God and why I serve Him every day."

She watched him as he dove into the conversation, chatting as if God were his best friend and he was immensely proud of his accomplishments. He talked about forgiveness, love, light, the commandments, how some folks find it difficult to follow them or just don't believe in them and why he finds them a necessity to live by.

"Bottom line, LuAnn, God knows the wrong you did that nearly killed Joci and Maddie and the pain to Jeremiah and the Sheppards, but He's already forgiven you."

"How can that be?"

"He loves you. Unconditionally. And He knows you're sorry and your heart is filled with remorse. I actually believe, He brought us together so I could share this with you. But,..." He leaned forward. "There's certainly no pressure. If you don't want to come to church, that's up to you, after all, I'm doing my job by speaking with you if we have our meetings. If you allow God to speak to you, you'll make your own decisions on whether you want to join us or not."

Judy came to the table carrying a tray with two of the biggest pieces of pie she'd ever seen. Piled high with whipped cream she thought she could have pieces of this pie for the rest of the week and still have some to share.

"Good grief, that's a huge piece of pie."

Judy beamed, "I make the tallest pies in town, guaranteed."

"That you do, Judy." Greg laughed and it was a pleasant sound. He was genuine.

"That all, Pastor?"

"Yes, ma'am, though I'll be honest and say you can bring me a box because likely a huge portion of this pie will come home with me."

"How about you, dear?"

"Yes, to a box for me as well, please."

"So, tell me, LuAnn, how are things at Forget Me Nots?"

She easily chatted about Forget Me Nots and how much she enjoyed working in the dirt and with the plants every day. She told him it brought her peace, and she went to bed each night tired but satisfied that she'd done good.

"This morning I was given the opportunity to create a custom bouquet for a lady who needed something quick to apologize to her friend for something silly she'd done. Her smile when I brought it out to her was the best payment I'd ever been given."

"There is something Godly about making people happy."

That felt like a sucker punch to her gut. It was the opposite of what she used to be like. In the past she'd been all about making herself feel better about things, not other people. That was likely her biggest mistake in all she'd done. But, how would she ever get them to realize that?

12

The air was warm as it blew around them. LuAnn's arms were wrapped tightly around his waist, her voluptuous breasts, soft, yet firm, pressed into his back, and it felt like...heaven. They were headed nowhere in particular, but nowhere felt right at this moment in time. No commitments, no restraints, no promises, just no. His heart and stomach had felt weighted down this afternoon after his conversation with Dog. He knew he had to broach the subject with her when they stopped. He knew just the spot.

Turning left and maneuvering to the road that led them along the river, he tried looking over as the sun, now lower in the sky, reflected orange across the water. The waves looked like orange diamonds floating along behind the million-dollar homes nestled among trees along some of the most prized real estate in Green Bay. The reflection of the setting sun on the water and then dancing off the windows of these immense estates added a whole new effect to the perfection of the night. Each time he thought about how he was about to mar its beauty, he quickly changed his thoughts to LuAnn behind him, holding him in a different way than she had in the past. Now it was more a feeling that she wanted to be this close to him, Chase, not that she needed to be with someone to prove how special she was. He didn't know if that was the correct way to describe it, but that's the best he could think of.

Slowing to turn into the small park on the east side of the river, he pulled in and was grateful the parking lot was semi full. If things went bad and the old LuAnn emerged from where she'd been hiding, and pitched a royal fit, there would be witnesses and someone to help out; in the alternative, she'd curb her swearing and bitching with so many people around. Either way, it suited him fine.

Finding a parking spot close to a picnic table, he pulled up to it, turned the bike so it faced the parking lot and was easier to pull out; he waited while LuAnn hopped off, dropped his kickstand, then dismounted himself.

"Want to sit here and watch the sunset?"

She turned and looked into his eyes, hers were clear, blue like a summer sky and gorgeous. Her dark hair had been pulled into a ponytail at her nape to keep it from snarling, the perfect fitting jeans were, well...perfect. The tank top she wore was white, nothing printed on it, and hugged her body in the most tantalizing way, but covered up her breasts, leaving only a hint of cleavage showing. It was enough to drive him wild.

"Sure." She smiled at him, then walked the few steps to the picnic table, climbed up on the bench and sat on the table facing the water. Her elbows rested on her knees; her body slightly bent forward with her hands clasped together as if in prayer.

"How was your meeting with Greg today? And, you don't have to tell me anything you don't want to. You know you never have to discuss your meetings with him."

He climbed up to sit beside her, close enough that their knees touched, but nothing more. They watched the water flow on by, still creating the mesmerizing flickers and glints, the sun now beginning to come closer to the horizon. In fifteen minutes, the sun would go down. It was breathtaking and awe inspiring.

"It was great. He's always so easy to talk to. Whenever I see him, I can see why you two are such good friends."

"He is, isn't he? No pressure. Great advice, while making you think it was your idea in the first place. And a great Pastor, too. Instead of preaching to you on Sundays, he's like the best storyteller. Making the bible seem like the book of a hundred stories, which is what it is, but he tells it in a way you can understand."

"I can see that. I think I'll go on Sunday and hear him firsthand."

Chase reached over and took LuAnn's hand in his and they sat for a long time watching the sun move ever closer to the horizon. A comfortable silence fell over them for a long time and he loathed to break it.

"I think it's great, LuAnn. I'd be happy to pick you up and bring you with me. We can ride with Greg after church and have lunch somewhere if you like."

She giggled and it sounded amazing. "I'd love to, but I don't want to take away your alone time with him."

He squeezed her hand then took a deep breath. "Rolling Thunder is in the last weeks of planning for the Veteran's Ride. I won't be available much in the next couple of weeks, so Sundays may be the only time we can get together. I hope you understand."

She was quiet for so long he turned his head to see if she'd heard him. Turning to him, just her head, not her body, she softly said, "Of course, I do."

Swallowing the nervousness that had risen to the top of his throat, he croaked out, "I'm sorry."

Clearing his throat, he hesitated before saying, "I'd bring you along if I could, LuAnn."

She lifted their linked hands to her lips and kissed his knuckles.

"I know you would, Chase. I certainly know why I can't be there. I'll keep myself otherwise occupied and it'll all be fine." Lifting his right hand, he cupped her jaw and kissed her lips. Softly. Just enough to taste her lips. He'd been thinking about them for so damned long.

She kissed him back, softly, eagerly, but not over the top. Just her soft full lips against his. His tongue dipped along her lips and he was surprised to feel her tongue dance along his. It was almost shy and reverent, and it felt like the first time in so many ways. For one, neither of them was drunk nor playing at just getting laid. This was different, he wanted her to enjoy kissing him. He wanted her to want him. He wanted her to want him as he'd always wanted her. Was that too much to ask?

13

In her mind, she knew this was the way it would be. She'd likely never be welcomed at Rolling Thunder, or its events, ever again. But, just now, hearing Chase more or less say it, well that just hurt. She gave herself a moment to ensure she wouldn't cry. She'd done enough of that over the past three years. Crying herself to sleep at night just to let it out. She'd cry in the bathroom sometimes, but mostly quietly in her bunk, because it was dangerous in prison to let the others see you cry. They'd dig and find your weakness and use it against you, sometimes physically, and she couldn't allow that, so she'd wait until deep in the night and smash her face into her pillow and let it all out.

Lost in her thoughts, she was surprised when he kissed her. It was so different this time. It was almost as if he were shy, or unsure of himself or maybe her reaction. In so many ways they were starting over now. They were both different people now. All the times they'd been together in the past, her head had been somewhere else on someone else. With Chase, she wasn't sure where his head had been.

He liked getting laid. She saw how other women looked at him. She'd begun recently to look at him in a different light. He'd filled out a bit since she'd been gone. His muscles were more defined, his back broader and solid. As they rode here and she pressed herself against him, she could feel how solid and muscular he was now. He'd spent a fair amount of time working out. His hair, still longer, brushed his shoulders. It was darker though, like he had it cut regularly and all the lighter sun-bleached ends were gone, which left dark, shiny, thick hair. His dark hair blended with his dark brown eyes, which had always been beautiful to look into, but now they held emotions in them other than having a crush on her. Sometimes she could almost see the emotions flowing through them. It was the most interesting thing to watch. His face, strong and classic, and she enjoyed the feel of the fine silky hairs as they brushed against her skin while their lips danced together. His scent wrapped around her and in a short moment, he filled her senses, all of them.

She kissed him back, enjoying the feel of his lips on hers. Her nipples pebbled as their tongues slid against each other. Emotions zinged around her body, creating goose flesh on her arms, and interesting feelings between her legs. She'd set sex aside for so long that she was surprised at the flush of emotions that whirled in her body and mind right now. It was dizzying. It was also exhilarating that those feelings were back again. She'd worried that she'd tucked them so far down they'd never surface again.

She and Chase had always been very sexual in the past. He liked sex the same way she did. Fast, hot, wild. Doubts and jealousy slipped into her mind and the thought that Chase very likely had not been celibate while she'd been locked away in prison came crashing down on her. Her eyes filled with tears even while their lips were touching.

She pulled away slightly and couldn't move fast enough to stop a tear that slid down her cheek before Chase saw it.

His thumb moved to her cheek and gently swiped away that errant little tear as his eyes looked directly into hers. He didn't say anything; he simply waited.

She inhaled and exhaled rapidly then softly said, "I wondered if you'd been with a lot of other women while I was away. You were always very sexual, and I can't blame you; you didn't owe me celibacy, but I did...do wonder."

He nodded slightly. "I've been with a couple. No one special. No one worth remembering."

She smiled but it was fake, she could feel that it was, but it was all she could do at this moment. "Understandable."

Slowly turning her head to see the sun now touching the water across from them, they sat in silence as the sun dipped into the water. It actually looked like it fell into the river and disappeared down below. Nature sure was interesting.

Chase had sat just as quietly as she, neither of them moving or saying anything further. Both of them likely afraid of what happened next. But she was getting used to that feeling, it was likely how her life would be from now on.

"Ready to head home?" His voice was gruff and filled with some unknown emotion. It was dark now and difficult to see his eyes.

"Yeah." She scooted off the table and stood. Walking to Chase's bike she pulled up the lid to the back tour pack and pulled a light sweater out. The air would be cooler now and usually the bugs came out in the dark, so it would keep her a little cleaner too.

Closing the lid, she waited as he climbed on his bike and nodded for her to get on the back. She did, but she held herself back instead of leaning forward and resting against him. A wall had just been erected between them and she wasn't sure why. They had no agreement when she went to prison. They weren't a couple, and based on the reason she went to prison, she had no business making any demands on anyone. It still hurt though. All of it. Rolling Thunder, Chase and other women. She should turn him loose completely so he could find someone that his friends would accept and not tear him apart over. But, that thought cut through her like a knife. Even though her possessiveness of Dog had resulted in a prison sentence, she decided to be possessive of Chase for a bit. She'd might get the courage to talk to Greg about it, too. He was good at giving advice and he knew Chase so well that would be just the thing to do.

14

His gut had clenched when she'd asked about other women. And, of course, there were a few. He'd said a couple and that was a bit of a lie. At first, he'd been with many. Trying to get LuAnn out of his mind and the anger and frustration of why she'd wanted Dog had torn him up. He'd defended her so many times to Dog and the others. He'd felt betrayed, used, abused and like a dumbass for sticking up for LuAnn and constantly bringing her along on rides. He'd just hoped that one of those times, she'd see him for him. The man he was.

Then, after a few months, he got sick and tired of banging sluts. No one had piqued his interest until he'd met Liv. Then there was always something stopping them from going out. She was with someone. He was busy. She was busy. Then he knew LuAnn would be getting out and he didn't want to start something that he wasn't sure his heart was a hundred percent in with.

Heading into the town's lights the closer they came to Green Bay, he blurted out, "Do you want to stop for ice cream?"

LuAnn giggled from behind him. "Sure, I haven't had ice cream in a long time."

Swallowing a knot that had just formed in his throat, he suddenly realized this might be the most foolish thing he'd do. Maybe ever. But, something compelled him to keep moving forward.

Turning right and getting off Winding Road that flowed along the river, he turned into town and closer to Lickety Split. The air had cooled considerably, but it was always good for ice cream. At least that's what he told himself.

As he neared the turn off to Lickety Split, his stomach tightened, and his heart raced. This was stupid. He didn't seem to have his head on straight at all tonight.

"Oh, that place is new." LuAnn said behind him.

"Yeah, it just opened a couple of years ago."

The parking lot was about half full while people sat around on the tailgates of their trucks, leaned against their cars and motorcycles, chatting and eating. The three picnic tables in front of the building were filled with customers and part of him thought that was a blessing. Liv would probably be too busy to notice he was here. And with someone at that.

Stopping his bike at the very edge of the parking lot between Lickety Split and the hardware store, he waited as LuAnn climbed off the back, then dropped the kickstand and dismounted. His legs actually shook a bit and he felt rather sheepish now that he'd put the three of them in this position.

"Did you want to stay here and let me get something for you?"

LuAnn looked up at him and smiled. "That's nice but I'd like to go and look at the menu. I'm not sure what they have here."

"Oh, just the usual ice cream kind of stuff."

"Okay, well, let's go look."

He hesitated and her head cocked to the left as she stared at him. "Is there a reason you don't want me to go up there with you?"

"No." It was a lie, and she must have been able to read it on his face because her smile fell like a rock.

"You know, you can just take me home, Chase. I don't want you to feel embarrassed."

"I'm not embarrassed, LuAnn." He took her hand, and they began walking to the large menu posted to the left of the order window.

They stood looking at the menu with three other people trying to decide what they'd like to order when it happened.

"Chase, it's so good to see you."

Her voice sounded genuinely happy to see him, then Olivia's eyes landed on LuAnn standing very close to him. Her eyes traveled down to their clasped hands then back up to his eyes, and her face said it all. He saw her swallow, then she cleared her throat and pasted on a fake smile before turning to LuAnn.

"Hi, my name is Olivia. I own Lickety Split."

LuAnn dropped his hand and held hers out to Olivia. "Hi. LuAnn. I'm a..." She turned to look at Chase clearly not sure how to describe herself. His throat seized up like an unoiled engine, and he could feel both LuAnn and Liv staring at him waiting for him to say something. LuAnn finished her sentence by saying. "I'm Chase's friend. It's nice to meet you."

The mood was dark. And heavy. Almost unbearably so. Then Liv spoke up first. "It's nice to meet you, LuAnn. The special flavor of the day is Pistachio Vanilla twist." Olivia looked at him once again, the control she was trying to keep in her voice clearly difficult. "I'll let you two decide what you want while I finish cleaning up the tables."

She quickly walked off and he could hear her greeting customers and trying to make small talk. Unsure of what he should or could say to LuAnn, he was saved. Sort of. By LuAnn herself.

"Is she one of the couple of women you spent time with?"

"No."

"It seemed rather awkward, Chase."

He turned to look into her eyes. He'd promised himself he would not lie to her, though he already had a little. Just to spare her and himself. Who was he kidding?

"I was attracted to Liv. Olivia. But it never seemed to work out, timing wise, for us to go out on a date, so we never did. But, I like her as a person. She's smart. Funny. And she's got a good head on her shoulders."

"And, she's beautiful. You left that part out." LuAnn said.

"Yes, she's beautiful."

"Why did you bring me here, Chase? Of all nights, after you mentioned that you'll be working a lot the next couple of weeks and I'm not welcome. Then, you bring me here to introduce me to someone you want to date but don't have or can't find the time to date. I honestly don't need this."

She pulled her phone out of her pocket. "I'll call a car to pick me up and you'll have the time right now to visit with Olivia."

He pulled the phone from her hand, took her hand in his and walked them to his bike. Then, he kept walking them across the empty hardware store parking lot. It was dark over there, secluded and it felt safe for some reason.

Leaning up against the four-foot-tall retaining wall, he turned to face LuAnn. He could see her face from the distant lights from the ice cream shoppe as his eyes adjusted to the light.

"Look, I'll admit to bad judgment and bad timing. It was stupid and not my best move to bring you to Liv's place tonight. But, something compelled me to do it. I needed to know that my feelings for you are stronger than my feelings for Liv. I've wrestled with this dilemma for over a year. Part of the reason I didn't ask her out right away was because of you. I dreamed of you at night. I thought about you during the day. All the time that you were away, the only thing I knew was that I had strong feelings for you, but you had strong feelings for someone else. I didn't know how to deal with that or about it."

She swallowed before she spoke and it took her a few moments to say anything at all, which made him so fucking nervous.

"Okay. That's fair."

She rubbed her left temple with her shaking fingers and continued, "That's extremely hard to admit and I thank you for telling me. But, I should tell you that after I went to prison, it didn't take me long to realize that my fixation on Dog was just that, a fixation. I didn't think about him at night when I went to sleep. I thought about you. I've puzzled over this for years now. I've tried to figure out my motives for my behavior. How could I have put you and Dog and Joci through all I did when I didn't love Dog. Not more than a brother like Lance. My possessiveness of Dog and jealousy of Dog and Joci was more fear of losing my place in the world, which was my job and our circle at Rolling Thunder. I guess I thought that at Rolling Thunder I was someone because I had a relationship of sorts with Dog because of Lance. I also didn't have a lot of friends that weren't associated with Rolling Thunder."

A tear slid down her cheek and she softly sniffed. "I'm

sorry, Chase. I don't know how a person gets so fucked up. I owe you an apology for the way I treated you; I embarrassed you in front of your friends, I used you for sex, and so many other things I did. I can't take it back; if I could, I would. But, I want you to know I'm very sorry and I'll never forgive myself for hurting you. I'll never hurt you like that again."

She began to blur in front of him and he wondered if he was having an attack of some sort, then realized, when a tear slid down his cheek, that he'd teared up. He opened his mouth to say something, accept her apology, anything but she spoke up first.

"I think the best thing I can do for you is let you go. You deserve so much more and clearly..." She turned her head toward the ice cream shoppe and Olivia who was chatting with customers. "You have someone you're interested in who doesn't make you carry all of her baggage. To the extent you ever had any, I release you from any responsibility you have for me."

15

She should have done that right away, but he was her anchor to this world outside of prison and her protector against Rolling Thunder. Being out here alone when she'd only ever known the Rolling Thunder gang as friends was scary. It was time to stop being afraid. She had to begin her life anew. It would be hard without Chase; he'd always been there for her. Even at her worst, he was there.

"LuAnn, I don't want to be released. I don't even know what that means."

She looked up into his beautiful dark brown eyes, so earnest, but now they looked confused.

"It means that if you and I ever have a chance at a real relationship, we have to build that on a foundation of trust, desire and love. It means you can't be here for me because you see me as a responsibility; it has to be because you truly want to be with me. I can't use you as a crutch to lean on whenever I need to be propped up. I have to be with you because I truly want to be, too. You don't deserve less than that. But, neither do I."

She watched his face as emotions moved across it at a rapid speed. His head bowed as he looked at the ground. Then, he raised his head and looked over at the ice cream shoppe. Olivia was just entering the side door with her hands full. He watched Liv for the briefest of moments, then looked at her again. His eyes were intense as they stared into hers. Looking into his handsome face made her heart break into a million little pieces. Why did doing the right thing always hurt so much?

"You don't get to decide for me. You've been doing that for years. I will decide for myself how things will be for me."

Had she been controlling him? God, she had. He'd always been open about the fact that he wanted to be with her, and she'd always used him and ignored his feelings. It was all about her. That realization made her stomach clench so tight that she thought she'd throw up.

"Okay. What do you want to do?"

He hesitated for the briefest of moments, before saying, "I want to take you home to my place and get to know your body all over again. I want to lay with you in my arms and I want to slide inside of you over and over again until we're both exhausted."

Shivers ran down her arms and moisture gathered between her legs. That sounded absolutely fantastic. She hadn't been with him in three years. Anyone. But, she hadn't wanted to be with anyone else.

"But," he said with a determination in his voice. "But, not until I know that you want the same from me. Me. Not Dog. Not anyone else. Me."

She lifted her right hand and lay it over his heart and felt the strong, solid and steady heartbeat beneath. Enjoying just touching him in this innocent manner, she waited a few seconds before interrupting the silence that now lay between them. Her mind ran in a thousand directions.

"How will I ever get you to understand that my fixation on Dog was merely an immature fear of not belonging, of losing the only world I had? I want you Chase Matthews, only you."

She watched his beautiful handsome face as he processed her words, the sweetest of smiles slowly formed on his face.

"But," she said with the same determination she'd heard in his voice. "But I need to know you want me and not Olivia or anyone else. Only me."

They were at a point where they needed to decide if they had a future with each other. And, there were so many unknowns before them. This was true of every couple, but their situation was likely more unknown than most. She wasn't welcome in his world, and her world was just beginning. The only friend she ever felt she had was Janice, but Janice worked at Rolling Thunder and hadn't contacted her since she'd gone to prison. So here she was, a clean slate with a dirty past. Joseph was right. She'd probably be better off moving on and going to a new state, a new town and really starting over. But, if there was one thing she knew about Chase, he loved it here. He loved Dog and JT, Ryder and Gunnar. He loved his job. And, now there was Greg. He knew how difficult it would be for both of them in Green Bay. His relationship with the guys at Rolling Thunder would never be the same if he continued to see her. He knew she would never be accepted by his "family" and life would be hard for her in Green Bay as an ex-con.

So, here they stood at a crossroads with an unknown future.

He stepped forward removing any space there'd been

between them. His arms wrapped around her and pulled her so close their torsos we're nearly one.

"If I kiss you now, the way I've wanted to kiss you since I picked you up a couple of weeks ago, will that show you?"

He hesitated just the briefest of moments, then continued, "How about if I take you over to the ice cream shoppe and kiss you in front of Olivia? Will that make you see that it's you I want?"

His lips touched hers, softly, molding together with hers as they both tested the fit. She cocked her head to the left the slightest little bit as his head cocked to the right and it was electric. The perfect fit of their lips together sent shivers down her body. He must have felt it too because his right hand came up and held her head in place as he deepened his kiss. His tongue, oh how she'd missed his tongue and the way it explored her mouth. The feel of the softness against her tongue as they mimicked love-making with their mouths. She felt him thicken and harden against her lower belly. His left hand roamed to her ass as he pulled her in closer to rub against his thickened cock.

Oh, how she'd missed that, too. Remembering the way he felt inside of her sent another riot of shivers through her body. And in that moment, she decided it didn't matter if they only had a few nights together and then they broke up, she'd at least have this for a while.

$\mathcal{Y}$ep, it was LuAnn he wanted. It had always been her. What he wrestled with was that she came with a truckload of baggage. Olivia seemed like the perfect no hassle partner. His head told him to pick Olivia. His heart and his body told him it was LuAnn.

As his lips devoured hers his heartbeat increased. She'd always revved him up. She used to dress trashier, her bountiful breasts usually strained to be free of whatever little scrap of shirt she wore, and she was tantalizing. But, now, she usually wore no makeup, her hair had lost all its blond coloring and again was the shiny, dark brown he'd admired when he picked her up at prison, which set off her crisp blue eyes. As he noticed at Linda's house the first time he saw her since dropping her off that first day, her clothing was greatly downplayed now, jeans and a t-shirt that covered her up. But, it worked. It all worked.

She had passion in her work at Forget Me Nots; and as he kissed her he could feel her passion for him. She was here with him.

They pulled away only a fraction from each other for

air; his forehead lay against hers and his voice was barely recognizable when he whispered.

"My place?"

"Yes."

His cock throbbed behind the course denim he wore, and he couldn't wait to shrug off the confinement. Riding home would be slightly painful, but the reward would make it worth it.

In unison they turned toward his bike and there stood Olivia watching them. He nodded at her, but she turned and walked back to the ice cream shoppe. LuAnn squeezed his hand and he looked down at her, the worry on her face was clear in the dim lights. He leaned down once again and kissed her lips.

"That took care of that."

"But..."

He tugged her along not sure what more to say about Olivia. He was glad she knew now where he stood, it made things a bit easier, though it was maybe a hurtful way for her to find out he'd made a decision to be with someone else. It wasn't intentional, but it was out now.

Tossing his leg over his bike seat, he sat, pulled his bike off the kickstand and looked over at LuAnn. She smiled at him and wasted no time climbing on behind him. She scooted close to him and her heat enveloped him as her arms circled around his waist. Her fantastic breasts pressed against his back and his cock twitched knowing what pleasures were to come.

He started his bike, put it into first gear and eased her out of the parking lot and onto the road to his home. It would be the first time LuAnn saw his home. He'd been so fucking proud the day he moved in, but for some reason, this felt like more. His chest swelled at the feeling of showing LuAnn what he'd managed to buy on his own. It wasn't palatial in any way, but it was a nice-sized house on a decent lot. He didn't have a fireplace inside, so he'd built a fire pit in the backyard and there'd been plenty of parties around the fire over the past couple of years.

He didn't have a cleaning lady, but he'd managed on his own. His lessons from hanging with Dog and the boys stuck with him. Get up in the morning and make your bed. Pick up your dirty clothes and once a week do your laundry, so you always have clean clothes. Other things like dusting he'd managed once every couple of weeks or so and he'd bought himself a little vacuum robot that ran every day while he was at work to vacuum the house. Though sometimes he had to go in search of her, it did keep the house moderately clean.

His excitement grew as they neared home and when he finally turned down his street his heartbeat sped up. He hoped she'd like his house.

He turned into the driveway and his sweet little ranch style home, illuminated by solar lights along the landscaping, looked homey and welcoming.

"Wow, Chase, this is amazing." LuAnn whispered in his ear and goosebumps raised on his arms. Reaching into a compartment on the dash of his bike, he tapped the garage door opener and smiled as his truck and Mustang came into view. As soon as the door opened enough for them to slip under, he pulled them into the garage and shut off the bike. LuAnn dismounted and he dropped the kickstand and climbed off. Taking LuAnn's hand, he walked to the door, which lead to a mud room, and then into the kitchen. Tapping the garage door button on the wall to close it, he opened the backdoor and held it allowing LuAnn to proceed him inside.

His mud room was where his shoes, boots and jackets all hung, and it was also where his washer and dryer were.

He had a laundry basket alongside the washer, half-filled with clothes but otherwise, it was rather neat.

"Very nice."

She looked around the room and his heart expanded that she was enthralled with his home.

"Thanks. Come see the rest of it."

He stepped out of the mud room and into the kitchen, his white maple cabinets setting off the tone for the rest of the room. Hardwood floors and white baseboards added the color contrast that lent itself to that homey feeling. He'd had granite counters installed seven months ago in a rich darker brown.

LuAnn looked around the room, her hand lovingly roamed over the granite as she took in the whole feel of the room. She turned and looked into his eyes, a soft smile on her face, and said, "This home is so you. It feels warm and comfortable and inviting. It's perfect."

He felt close to combusting at her praise and his throat felt tight. Rather than trying to say something, he pulled her into his arms and his lips brushed against hers. At first he meant to be soft, but the second their mouths joined, his head stopped thinking. At least the head on his shoulders did.

His hands roamed down to the bottom of her shirt and began pulling it up, only releasing her mouth long enough to pull her shirt over her head, then his lips consumed hers once again. Without thought his fingers unfastened her bra and he felt the weight of her breasts as they fell against him and his cock pained him inside the confines of his jeans.

LuAnn's fingers shook as she began unfastening the button on his jeans and as soon as she'd undone it, she deftly lowered his zipper, and the relief was immediate and needed. She didn't stop there though; her hands began pushing his jeans down his hips and to the floor. She held his jeans as he stepped free from them and while she was down there, she looked up at him as she lowered his briefs, a sassy smile on her lips as she lowered them over his hard cock. As it bobbed free, she took it in her mouth and his knees damned near buckled from the feel of her hot, wet mouth taking him inside her. Her head bobbed up and down and her wet mouth sucked his cock, her right hand at the base pumped in rhythm with her mouth. Her left hand cupped his balls and stars danced before his eyes.

Three fucking years he'd waited for this. LuAnn's mouth was expert on his cock. She could make him come so fucking fast sometimes and then others, when she was feeling playful, she could prolong it to the point he'd almost beg her for release.

His left hand lay on the top of her head and he added pressure to it when she neared the tip of his cock, not wanting to lose the feel of her mouth on him. She moaned and the vibration of it sent chills down his spine as he felt the precum form at the tip of his cock. Her tongue sweetly swiped over it and she moaned again, and his breathing started coming in spurts and puffs rather than regular breaths.

"Lu..."

Her hand tightened at the base of his cock and she began pumping faster, her mouth sucking firmer, and he had to lean over and rest his hand on the counter for fear of falling over.

"Jesus..."

She moaned again, and then again, knowing how he liked it and just like a volcano erupting, his seed spewed forth and she sucked down every drop, making sure to clean him up with her tongue as his cock softened in her mouth.

Once his vision came back, he stepped back, lifted her

under her arms till she stood before him, then he picked her up and tossed her over his shoulder as she shrieked and laughed, and he hauled her down the hall to his bedroom.

Laying her on the bed, he quickly unfastened her button, slid the zipper of her jeans down and quickly jerked her jeans down her sexy long legs. Tossing them to the floor he reached forward and ripped her panties off, the tear of the fabric causing her to gasp. He'd always wanted to do that to her. She made him feel wild.

He bent down and fit his mouth over her clit and immediately sucked her into his mouth. Flicking her with his tongue her gasp made him bolder, wilder, freer. He slid his forefinger into her warmth and her legs immediately spread open for him. He kneeled on the floor, and scooted her to the edge of the bed, at the perfect height for his mouth to make her come. Her legs lay over his shoulders, his mouth fit perfectly over her pussy, his tongue flicking and licking, his fingers plunging into her channel, her gasps and moans coming faster and faster and she cried out his name and her juices poured out on his tongue.

He softened his mouth on her as she twitched when he hit a tender spot, her breathing beginning to slow, her body limp from her orgasm.

Slowly, he rose up, sat on the bed and pulled her up to him, then his mouth once again covered her lips as his hands began squeezing, lifting, playing with those breasts he'd dreamed about so often.

17

That had been everything she'd been dreaming of all of her time away. Probably better because it was real. Chase had always been an expert lover. He always wanted her to come when they had sex; he wasn't in the least selfish, but caring and sexy. God she'd been so incredibly stupid. How could someone be so blind?

She lay there in his arms, both of them beginning to recover from their recent orgasms, Chase fondling her breasts, his breathing beginning to increase. His cock grew thick and full. She watched as the simple act of playing with her breasts aroused him. Unable to resist touching him, she lay her right hand on his cock, and rubbed it softly, enjoying the softness of his skin pulled tighter and tighter as he continued to grow.

He switched positions quickly and without forewarning, hovered over her, a sexy smile on his face, his cock between her legs. His lips once again mastered her lips, the delicious weight of his body warming her and the twitching of his cock between her legs bringing wetness to that same region. Lifting her hips, she felt the tip of his cock against her curls and he groaned against her lips.

He stretched to the side, pulled open a drawer on a night table and pulled a condom from the drawer. Lifting his head a fraction and turning to the side, he ripped the package open with his teeth, pulled the condom from the package, then planted his lips against hers as his hips raised and he rolled the condom on in record time.

Her legs spread open further and he huffed, "God damn you're sexy, Lu."

She managed to answer between kisses, "So are you, Chase."

Then his amazing cock slipped inside her body. He lifted his head and looked down into her eyes as he moved out and back in a few times. The feeling was exquisite, his body fit perfectly as he filled her again and again. She was already slightly tender from his earlier ministrations and when he put pressure on her clit by rubbing against her, she lifted her hips to allow him to slip in further. Electric.

Their bodies moved together, move for move, each bringing the other to their ultimate conclusion. It had never felt better. It had never felt so right. It had never been like this. This was perfection.

Her hands roamed over his back, the muscles bunching and stretching as his hips slammed inside then pulled out only to do it again. Their bodies formed a fine sheen of sweat as they warmed from their exertion; her heart raced as her body enjoyed his body, his weight, his breathing. Just him.

He groaned and pushed tightly against her, swirled his hips then his voice cracked as he whispered, "I need you to come, Lu. I'm almost there. Swear to God."

She lifted her legs and wrapped them around his ass, and he groaned again, and his pace increased as his muscles began to quiver. He was trying to hold back for her. She thrust herself against him a couple of times and her orgasm hit her like a truck. She cried out his name and he managed to huff out. "Thank. Fuck." He pumped only twice more and strained as he held himself inside of her as his orgasm hit.

He lay on her, not his full weight, but a fair amount of it and it felt fantastic. Her heart felt full and she stifled a giggle by closing her eyes and listening to Chase's breathing in her ear.

After a few moments, he pulled out of her, took the condom off and tossed it in the wastebasket on the side of the bed. Laying on his back, he pulled her to him, his left arm under her neck, his right arm pulling her close. She let out a deep breath and settled herself into him and fell fast asleep.

Waking later to Chase's deep breathing she lay staring in the dark enjoying this quiet, peaceful feeling. It was the most serene she'd felt in three years. Her life was far from perfect, that was an understatement. But she'd take this little bit of peace and fill her soul with this moment to last her for any rough days ahead.

"What are you thinking about?" His voice was deep and sleep laden and sexy as hell.

"This."

A deep rumble rolled through his chest and he repeated her word. "This."

He rolled to his side and looked down at her. She could see the features in his face, though they were darkened in the room, but she knew how handsome he was. What she couldn't make out due to the lack of light, she filled in with her memory of how handsome he was.

"This is pretty special isn't it?" His voice held only a hint of humor. "My heart hasn't felt this sated in years."

She lay her left hand over his heart and felt the strong even beat of it. The sadness that threatened to creep in was pushed away quickly; she didn't want this moment to end so soon. There'd be plenty of time to beat herself up later.

"Mine, either." She took a deep breath, breathing in Chase and their mingled aroma. "I want it to last just a bit longer."

"Then stay tonight. I'll get you home in plenty of time for work tomorrow."

Chills ran down her spine and she quickly replied, "I'd love that."

Her response earned her his lips on hers once again and his body moving closer to hers. Perfection.

18

The following week passed slowly. Chase's schedule consisted of work, Veteran's Ride planning, going home and falling dog-ass tired to sleep only to start it over again. He missed her. He missed LuAnn. Her smile, her new even demeanor. Of course, her body. He'd thought about calling her a hundred times but then someone would interrupt him, or he'd have to finish something up. It didn't help that he felt awkward calling her from Rolling Thunder. He could take the shit he'd get, but he just didn't need the bullshit right now.

Ryder hollered from the shop door, "Chase, there's a guy on the phone who wants to talk to you. He won't give his name, says it's important."

Setting his wrench on the work bench, Chase walked to the shop office while wiping his hands on the shop rag permanently tucked into his back pocket. Entering the office Ryder nodded to him, and whispered, "Persistent fucker." Then left the office so Chase was alone.

Picking up the phone and pushing the button on the

blinking light on the phone, he answered, "Chase Matthews."

"Chase this is Gil Jones with Chief's Cycles. I've wanted to touch base with you for a while now. One of my guys, Derek, met you in Sturgis last year and he told me about your mad skills with bike designs. How would you feel about coming out here to my place in Colorado and chatting with me about working for me as my head bike designer?"

His mind went blank for a moment. What?

Finally finding his voice, Chase responded, "Wow, first of all, I'm flattered, but is this a joke?"

Gil laughed; his deep belly laugh sounded genuine. "No, Chase, this isn't a joke. My place is growing by leaps and bounds and Derek is a huge fan of yours. He's showed me some of the designs you've created. Before you say anything more, I know you largely work with JT and I also know that JT shared some of the bikes you created on your own with Derek while they had a few beers. I know you have talent. I've looked up a couple of the bikes you built and looked at them myself in person. You have incredible skills and I'd love for you to work for me here in Durango."

Chase sat hard in the desk chair that faced a large window which peered into the shop. Employees of Rolling Thunder, his friends, were out there working. The shop was neat and clean, his friends were friends for life. He hoped.

"I have to tell you I'm flattered, Gil. But, it has never occurred to me that I'd leave here one day. Dog has been like a father to me."

"I do understand, but let's be real for a moment. JT is Dog's son. He's the Head Designer there and it wouldn't matter if you created the best damned motorcycle in the world, you'll never be Head Designer at Rolling Thunder. Blood is thicker than water as they say. And that is nothing against Dog or JT, it's just the honest to God truth."

Shoveling his hand through his hair, Chase stared out the window. It was certainly intriguing but...

"Thank you so much for thinking of me, but I just have to decline. I'm set up here, own a house, family, a girl, the works."

"I'll leave it at this, Chase. Think about it. I can take care of getting your house sold. Your girl can come here and work either at Chief's or somewhere else if she wants. We have jobs. You never know how things will change, so let's just say we'll touch base in a few weeks."

"Sure. That sounds good and thank you."

"You bet. Talk to you soon."

The line went dead, and Chase's head spun. That was out of the blue.

The door opened and Dog walked in.

"Chase, the Garrett's called and are wondering if things are on schedule with their bike. Can you give me an update?"

Guilt washed over him as Dog stood before him. He didn't initiate that phone call, but in a small way, he'd been talking about him with someone else and that felt rather disloyal at the moment. He could feel the heat color his cheeks as he stood to face Dog.

"Yeah, I think things are on schedule. The only fly in the ointment is that the exhaust system still hasn't been delivered, but I'll give them a call right now and see if it's coming soon or if we have to go a different route."

Dog nodded. "If you can't get anywhere with them, JT can call them, too, he's built a great relationship with Chip over there."

Dog turned and left and that disloyal feeling in his stomach turned into acid. He'd also built a nice relationship with Chip at Samson's Exhaust and damn it he didn't need JT undermining him.

Sitting back down at the desk he shook the mouse on the computer to wake it up, then typed in Samson's Exhaust and found his order and the phone number.

Dialing the number, he tamped down the bitterness that had settled in his stomach and told himself he was just being oversensitive. He'd call LuAnn tonight and spend some time with her that would soothe him. He wanted to touch her and be with her. Now that he'd had a taste of her again, he wanted more and more.

Finishing up his call and happy that things were still on track, Chase walked to his workstation where Gunnar and Ryder were waiting for him. That same guilt settled in his stomach as he approached the brothers, but he reminded himself that he didn't call Gil. It was the other way around and had nothing to do with him being disloyal. But it sure felt like it.

Gunnar turned and smiled. "So, Veteran's Ride is next weekend and our bachelor party the following weekend. Are you ready for all of the fun?"

"I'm as ready as I can be. Just tell me where to be for the bachelor party and I'm there."

They laughed and he could tell they wanted to say more, and he had a suspicion he knew what that was, or more accurately, who it was about, but he didn't give them the time to say anything and piss him off. Instead, he said, "I can't believe two hot women like Molly and Emma even want you sad sacks."

Gunnar laughed. "That's the mother of my son you're talking about, asshole."

Chase laughed, picked up his wrench and began

working on the bike for the Garretts while Ryder and Gunnar walked away talking about some wedding bullshit the girls had them doing. He knew he'd have to attend the double wedding, but he felt awful about not being able to bring LuAnn. She'd likely feel pretty shitty about it, too.

19

Turning the metal bucket, to and fro, LuAnn added a few touches of purple Ophelia and Lavender to the purple and white roses she'd already inserted into the bucket. Finishing the unique arrangement with a sweet purple bow, she smiled and admired her masterpiece before she pulled her phone from her back pocket and snapped a picture of it. This was certainly one for her photo album!

Tucking her phone back into her pocket, she picked up the tin bucket and walked to the counter where her customer stood waiting for it.

"Oh my." The sweet gray-haired woman exclaimed. "That is simply perfection."

She could feel her cheeks turn warm from the praise. "Thank you."

The customer turned the bucket back and forth looking at all sides. "This is the prettiest centerpiece I've ever seen."

LuAnn simply smiled. Would she ever get enough of the praise she received for her floral arrangements? It was a bonus that she loved working with the colorful, fragrant flowers. It was an even bigger bonus that she'd learned to grow them. From this point forward, no matter where she ended up in life, she had this and always would.

"LuAnn." She turned at the sound of her name. A familiar looking woman in her mid-forties approached. Her dark hair was streaked with gray which glinted in the sunlight. She wore jeans and a white t-shirt, which was smudged with dirt and grime that came from working in the soil and with plants.

"Yes," She answered.

"Hi, LuAnn. I wanted to introduce myself. I'm Lily, Jan is my mom and Luke is my stepfather. I've been away attending to a family issue on my husband's side, but I'm back now and wanted to meet you. I've been hearing all good things about you."

"It's nice to meet you. Jan mentioned she had a daughter who worked here." The resemblance was remarkable. She looked like a younger version of Jan.

Lily laughed and looked around the back of the shop. "You're keeping things clean and orderly and I can't tell you how important that is to us."

"Oh, well, I like being able to find things. I'm glad it works for both of us."

"Excuse me?"

She turned to see another customer at the counter and looked back at Lily, "Excuse me, I need to take care of our customer."

Lily nodded her head and turned to leave.

Turning to the new customer, LuAnn greeted her, "Hi, how can I help you?"

"I'm looking for something unusual for my dinner party next week." She put dinner party in air quotes.

Laughing LuAnn looked this woman in the eye. "Tell

me how unusual and what this party is for, then we'll come up with something spectacular together."

The woman looked around the shop at various displays and containers before responding.

"I play Bridge and I'm hostessing our annual dinner party this year next Saturday. These women are dear friends but, dare I say, we've gotten into a bit of "table wars" over the years, each one trying to out-do the last. I want something to place in the middle of the gift table that no one else can get, so rare and unusual and I'll add, money isn't an object. I'd sell a lung to see these bitches' jaws drop. Friendly speaking that is."

She laughed but the glint in her eyes said it all. Turning to the back counter, LuAnn pulled the catalogue of flowers from the shelf, lay it open on the counter between the customer and herself and opened it up to some of the unusual flowers she'd been reading up on lately. Finding just what she wanted, she turned the catalogue so her customer could see it, pointed to the Fritillia and Lysichiton and their bold green, orange and yellow colors and the woman gasped.

"That's perfect." She leaned down closer to the catalogue and stared at the flowers together. "What type of container would you put these in?"

"Tell me, you said dinner party, is that formal, whimsical, or rustic?"

LuAnn watched the slow smile crawl across the woman's attractive face. Her green eyes glinted as if there were an actual light coming from them. "Rustic all the way. I've told everyone to wear outdoor clothing as in garden party or bar-b-que. Everyone else has done stuffy formal gatherings. I'm doing a guess your plate event."

Laughing at this woman's excitement, she asked, "Oh my, what is a guess your plate event?"

"I'm making up words for all the things that might be included in a meal. There will be a menu, and we're doing roast pig, as in an actual pig roast, baked beans, coleslaw, biscuits, potatoes, green beans, etc. There will be made up words for each item including utensils, cups and napkins. Everything will be served in courses. So, attendees will see a menu, then will be given a list of the made-up names/words and they'll pick three items per course. They won't know what those items are until they're served. So, you might order green beans, a knife and a biscuit. Next course will be the same. It's so fun watching people try to guess what each thing is after the first course is served. Guests begin to share what they ordered and then look at each other's plates. Someone might get all food and no utensils. It's all a gamble. But it sure gets people laughing and having fun."

Now LuAnn was laughing just thinking of the fun, and maybe chaos that might ensue if someone didn't have a sense of humor about it all.

"Okay, so we can either use a hollowed-out log as a container, or if you want something that looks more bar-b-que-esque, we could use an old, speckled coffee pot or an old pot. It'll all depend on what I can find."

"Yes. Yes. Yes. That sounds perfect. Make it large, I'll put it on the side table along with little gifts I'm giving to each guest. It'll certainly make a statement. Then, what do I have to pay you to not use these same flowers again for a year."

Laughing she shrugged. "I can't guarantee that no one else will use them, so I hate to take your money on that. But, I can tell you, I'm likely the only one here that enjoys studying unusual and rare flowers, so there's that. And, you can make up a name for the flowers, so no one really knows what they are."

"Splendid." The customer shrieked and clapped her hands.

LuAnn wrote her order down, rang it up and the woman paid for half to get the order started.

Once the lady left the store, LuAnn called her supplier to see if she could get the Fritillia and Lysichiton. Promised by her supplier that they had someone who specialized in the unique, LuAnn hung up, pulled her phone from her back pocket and scheduled a reminder to call the supplier back in the morning to check on progress.

"That was fantastic, LuAnn."

Jumping, her cheeks and ears burned at being caught on her phone and her brain didn't quite register what Lily had said.

"I'm sorry, I was just setting a reminder to call the supplier in the morning to check on this order."

Lily laughed. "No need to apologize, the way you handled Mrs. Smythe was lovely. She's a very good customer and you made her tremendously happy."

"Oh, thank you." Her cheeks burned brighter; she felt the heat on her chest as well as up her neck.

"I'd love it if you would help us at the farmers market on Wednesday evenings. If you're available. You can have half a day off on Fridays to make up for the extra time you'll be spending there. I think our customers would be thrilled with your sense of style and service."

Her heartbeat increased as she let the praise and words sink in. She'd wondered about the farmers market after she overheard a couple of the employees chatting about them and how much it had helped Forget Me Nots growth over the years. They'd said it was an honor to be asked to represent the store there.

"I..." She swallowed and shook the daze from her brain. "I'd love to, yes."

Being there would give her the opportunity to show off some of the artistry she'd learned and help her learn more as she had the opportunity to work on creating fantastic bouquets and arrangements for customers.

Lily grinned and clapped her hands in front of her. "We start tomorrow night. Once you've finished with these custom orders come on back and we'll go over how we manage the farmers market."

"I'll be back there in a little while."

She watched as Lily walked to the greenhouse. She couldn't help the smile that creased her face. She was excited to tell Chase. At least when she saw him next. She knew he was busy, but the self-doubts crept in the longer time passed and she didn't see him. In the middle of the night, she'd lay awake and wonder if he'd decided to move on. Maybe she was just too hard to build a relationship with after all. Surely the crew at Rolling Thunder was filling his brain with negative thoughts about her. Then she'd tell herself that this was Rolling Thunder's biggest event of the year and every employee worked extra hard during the weeks leading up to the Veteran's Ride. Satisfied with her explanation, she'd finally roll over and fall asleep.

Maybe she'd send him a text. That wasn't too intrusive. He could respond when he had a minute.

20

Rereading the text before he sent it, Chase examined his words.

'Do you want to go for a ride tonight?'

He didn't want to sound pushy or needy, but he missed her. Taping "send" he sat back on his sofa and took a deep breath.

His stomach growled and he sat up, looked toward his kitchen and mumbled, "Shit."

He hadn't had time this past week and a half to do anything and that included grocery shop. Pulling his phone off his lap, he scrolled the internet for a restaurant that delivered. He'd order, then shower and wait for LuAnn to respond to his text. If she did.

Greg had told him this week that LuAnn had called and said she picked up a Sunday morning shift at work and wouldn't be at church. His heart plummeted when he heard that for a couple of reasons. Why didn't LuAnn tell him that? Even if by text. And, he had been disappointed that he wouldn't see her. So he went to church trying to keep his eyes from scanning the congregation and looking like a psycho, then he returned to Rolling Thunder. He finished up working on sign stands for the parking for this coming weekend. There were only three more days until the Veteran's Ride. If he couldn't see LuAnn before the Ride, he'd hopefully see her after. And, he knew he'd have to tell her he was going to the weddings without her, another thing which would hurt her so he could be with his "family." His stomach twisted again, which seemed to be the norm these days.

Tapping on a restaurant icon, he ordered his meal via the app, paid for the food and delivery, then walked to his bathroom and turned on the water in the shower. He was ready to wash this day away. He'd had a rollercoaster of emotions today and there was the promise of more to come.

Stepping from his shower, Chase towel dried his hair, swiped the towel down his body and walked into his bedroom. Stepping into his briefs, then jeans, he grabbed a clean t-shirt and slipped it over his head as he walked to the front of the house. His doorbell rang and his stomach growled again.

Turning to the front door, he opened it to see a young pimple-faced boy standing at his door with a bag in his hand. A quick glance at the car in the driveway told him this kid wasn't making a financial killing in the delivery business. Reaching to his wallet, Chase pulled out a five-dollar bill and handed it to him.

"Thanks." The kid said with a grin on his face.

"Thank you." Chase took his food bag and stepped into the house, closing and locking the door behind him. The aroma of a grilled hamburger and steaming french fries surrounded him and his mouth actually watered. Walking into the kitchen, he reached into the bag and pulled out a few fries, popping the potatoes in his mouth. As he chewed, he walked to the refrigerator and pulled out a beer. He had to be back at Rolling Thunder in an hour, but that didn't stop him from thinking he'd love to take a nap right now. After filling his gut with tasty food and a beer or two.

While moving the bag of hot food to the kitchen table his phone chimed, and he naturally reached back for it only to find his pocket empty. Looking up and into the living room he saw his phone laying on the coffee table and walked in to retrieve it.

His heartbeat sped up when he saw LuAnn's name.

"Hey there, just got your text. I have to work late tonight to help pack up for the farmers market tomorrow. I miss you." The sentence ended with a red heart and the excitement he felt was ridiculously immature for a man his age. But, still he was happy to hear from her.

Walking into his kitchen and sitting at the table, he quickly typed out a message back to her.

"I do, too, but would like to see you. Later? Tomorrow?"

"I have to work tomorrow, too. Maybe after the Veteran's Ride?"

"It's a date. I'll pick you up at 7:00."

"I can't wait."

He stared at the words for a few minutes, then set his phone on the table. All of his news would have to wait until Saturday. He pulled the hamburger from the bag, unwrapped it and devoured it quickly. Sitting back in his chair, he swallowed the last bite, took a long pull of his beer, then looked at his phone. He easily had forty-five minutes before he had to be at Rolling Thunder, so he tapped the alarm app on his phone, set the alarm to wake him in a half hour, walked into the living room and flopped back on the sofa. He was beginning to hate this living between two worlds. It was only going to get tougher as the weddings approached.

Just before drifting off to sleep he had a vision of a bike. The gas tank was sleek and stretched. The color escaped his imagination this time, but as was the norm for him, it would come. Dreaming up new designs was pure joy. The bike's handlebars stretched back over the tank smoothly as if they hovered over the tank to both protect it and add dimension. The seat flowed seamlessly from under the driver to the back fender, not adding bulk, but fitting the lines of the bike. It would have to be custom-made. The back fender extended from under the seat, and it sexily flowed over the back tire and halfway down to the road. It was cut in a curve at the end to keep any of the lines from being blunt or harsh. Just as he drifted off to sleep the color came to him. Blue...like LuAnn's eyes.

Excitement was an understatement for her feelings. She'd had a great day today. The sample flowers she'd ordered for Mrs. Smythe had been delivered and she mocked up an arrangement in the speckled coffee pot she'd found at a local craft store on her lunch hour. Lily had been eager to see the flowers placed together and come to life. LuAnn was so thrilled that she took a picture of the mini arrangement and sent it to the vendor to show her contact there, Jasmine, what she planned on doing. Jasmine immediately sent a text back telling her how magnificent it was. Just that one compliment had her day soaring into the top compliment category of her best days.

It was her first farmers market and as she was unpacking her enthusiasm increased. The excitement of her fellow vendors chatting, setting up their booths and the warm, beautiful weather made this day damned near perfect. It would be perfection if she were able to see Chase tonight. But, she wasn't sure what time she'd be finished, and she knew he was working his tail off getting ready for the ride this weekend. Feeling bad about sticking him in the middle between her and the Rolling Thunder crew, she'd decided it was likely best if she didn't see him during this time. She didn't want him to feel pushed or pulled in either direction. At least not by her doing. Hadn't she already learned that lesson the hard way.

"Hi, are you open for business yet?"

She turned to see a young woman with a small child standing at her table looking over the flowers she'd brought with her. She had both premade bouquets of flowers, and individual flowers so she could customize one if the customer wanted one.

"Sure, how can I help you?"

"I'd like that bouquet right there." She said pointing and LuAnn promptly pulled it from the water bin she had it sitting in and wrapped the stems in plastic before taking the woman's money. This began a non-stop evening of selling, creating, and cashing out customers, that blew by quickly. Joseph was there replenishing the flowers from the store truck as she sold them, but she admitted to herself, they could have used another employee to take the money. She'd worked her tail off. The first time she had to look at her phone to check the time was three hours later. Only an hour to go at the market, but she'd have to get the unsold flowers back to the greenhouse and take the money to the safe. So, she still had easily a couple hours to go.

"Hi there. Are those Calla Lilies?"

Tucking her phone in her pocket as her embarrassment flushed up her neck and cheeks, she turned to see two beautiful young women standing at her booth pointing to some of the sample flowers she'd gotten from her vendor along with Mrs. Smythe's.

"Oh, they are. They are called Aqua Blue Purple Picasso Calla Lilies. They are quite rare, but I have a vendor who knows my penchant for the unusual."

The dark-haired woman smiled as she stared at the gorgeous lilies Joseph had just unloaded from the truck.

"Those are seriously the most gorgeous flowers I've ever seen."

LuAnn smiled, "Would you like me to pull them together with some greens and baby's breath?"

The blond woman giggled. "Absolutely. Can you make two bouquets with them?"

Smiling, LuAnn responded, "You bet I can."

She turned to pull the lilies from the water container they sat in, but her eyes landed on Chase. There he stood a couple of booths down from her. First her eyes drank him in. He looked especially sexy tonight. His long, tall frame was encased in nice fitting jeans, his biker boots and a dark t-shirt he had tucked into those jeans which showed off his lean, muscular, physique so damned well. Then he laughed and her eyes landed on the woman chatting with him. It was none other than Olivia. He was here with Olivia. Of course, she looked gorgeous. Her long, blond hair hung over her shoulders and her tight jeans showed how toned and in shape she was. The t-shirt she wore hugged her curves and left very little to the imagination. Her cleavage was on display much like LuAnn used to dress in her former life. Chase had been attracted to her then. So, nothing had really changed as far as he was concerned. He still liked the tight clothes and the show 'em off look.

Feeling her fingers squeezing the lilies, she held she forced herself to remember her place here. Though her fingers shook, she pulled together two pretty, yet different arrangements with the Calla Lilies and both women seemed thrilled with their floral choices.

"Mama, those are so pretty."

A little girl, around seven years old with blond, curly

hair had come to stand between the women, but her pretty blue eyes landed on the flowers.

"They are, aren't they? Where's Maddy?"

"She's over by Grandpa."

"Okay." The blond woman looked at her a smile on her face. "I can't wait to show my husband-to-be this arrangement. We've been boring our fiancés to death with talk of flowers and the like. I'm sorry we already have our wedding florist selected and paid for; I love what you do here."

Trying to get her head back in the game, LuAnn swallowed the disappointment and fear in her throat and plastered on a smile.

"Thank you." Remembering business first, she reached down and pulled out a business card for Forget Me Nots and handed one to each of the women. "Here's our business card. If anything changes, please give us a try." She smiled in return. "The bouquets are $20 each."

"Thank you." The dark-haired woman said as she took the card from LuAnn's hand.

"What are you two buying now?" A familiar male voice asked.

Dread filled LuAnn's stomach as she slowly looked up to see Gunnar Sheppard standing before her. He carried a little boy, around two years old in his arms and the blond woman turned to him and smiled.

"We've found the most beautiful flowers here. Look!" She exclaimed.

Gunnar looked at the flowers and smiled, then tapped the end of her nose with his forefinger. "Still not as beautiful as you, Em."

His eyes then looked at LuAnn and she wanted to sink into the concrete at the pure evil that transformed his usually handsome face. He stared for a few moments. It felt like forever. When he finally spoke, his voice held nothing but venom.

"You have got to be shitting me."

Not sure what to do or where to go and not wanting this to become a horrible nightmare, she stood straight, pulled her shoulders back and waited for him to say more. Instead, Chase quickly came over and tried diffusing the situation.

"Gunnar. Not here. Not now."

Gunnar continued to stare at her and even though her knees shook, she stood still mostly because she wasn't sure what to do. She didn't want things to get worse, but she was totally unsure about what to do.

"Gunnar." Chase scolded.

Finally, Gunnar looked at Chase, then at the woman he called Em and said, "Let's get out of here."

Both women looked confused but sheepishly smiled at her, took their flowers and laid their $20 each on the table between them and walked away with Gunnar.

Chase turned to her, "Are you alright?"

"Yes." Her voice shook. Her whole body shook now. Eventually she'd have to see them all. It was a given that she'd run into them somewhere. The grocery store, or hardware store, or with Chase. Even though she'd just seen Chase with Olivia and her heart was breaking, she was so happy he was there. Unable to look at him she picked up the money on the table and tucked it under the table in the money box she used.

Taking in a huge breath, she let it out slowly.

"Um, thank you for coming over. I was shocked to see him and apparently him me, but I'm glad you were here to keep things from getting ugly."

"Of course, I'd never let any of them hurt you."

She nodded, then turned to pick up flowers and redistribute them in the water bins they rested in. Anything to keep busy.

"Hey." Chase's voice was soft. "Can you look at me?"

Lightly clearing her throat, she stopped fussing and turned to face him. Hesitating, she drew in another deep breath and slowly looked up into his eyes.

"Why are you hesitant to look at me?"

Her eyes looked past him, but Olivia wasn't there.

"I saw you. With her. Olivia. I assumed you were on a date."

"We aren't. She happened to be here. We've been busting ass at the shop all week. The past two weeks actually, I told you that. We came down here tonight because Dog wanted us to pick up some things from the sign shop for the ride this weekend. The girls, Molly and Emma, Ryder and Gunnar's fiancés, wanted to stop to pick up a few things. Veggies and whatnot. Olivia just happened to be at the market and yes, I stopped to talk to her. I'm not rude."

Tears sprang to her eyes. She'd run into a Sheppard, which had damned near knocked her over, she thought Chase was with someone else and now she felt the fool. What had started out as a great day had sure gone to hell in a handbasket in a nanosecond.

"I'm..." Sniffing she tucked a wayward lock of hair behind her ear and tried again. "I'm so sorry. I've thought about you so much and I miss you. I'm so self-conscious and you deserve better."

That last part came out without thought. She shocked herself for saying it. But she knew it was true.

"I deserve the person who makes my heart race and my body respond. I deserve the person I want to be with and who wants to be with me. I know this is hard right now, but it'll get better."

He stepped closer to her and she watched his jaw twitch. "I want you, LuAnn."

His lips touched hers lightly and she felt the thrill of it to her toes.

"Well, look at this."

She jumped at the man's voice and turned to see Ryder Sheppard standing at the table.

"Gunnar told me you were here, and you looked different. I had to stop and see for myself. I had no idea you two were an item."

While his voice didn't hold nearly the malice that Gunnar's had, it was tight.

"Who I'm with isn't your concern, Ryder. Seriously, let's not make this an issue."

Ryder nodded once. "I know, Chase, I'm just surprised is all. I mean, I knew you stayed in contact, I just didn't know it was this close contact."

LuAnn watched Chase's face. His eyes locked on Ryder's and while they weren't posturing as if they would fight, there was tension in the air.

"Again, the closeness of the contact is none of your concern."

Ryder nodded and took a step back. His green eyes swiveled to hers and held for a moment. Just before turning, he said, "See you at the shop."

Chase stood stock still for a time after Ryder walked away and LuAnn felt horrible. This would no doubt create extreme tension for Chase at work and that was the last thing she wanted for him.

After a few moments, Chase inhaled deeply and let it out in a whoosh. "Well, now the word is out, so no more hiding it from anyone."

"I'm so sorry, Chase."

"Nope, Lu, it actually feels like a relief. I wasn't quite

sure how to bring it up without the possibility of all hell breaking loose. Even though comments will be made, and things will be different, I'm glad it's out there now."

Her head tilted back to look up into his eyes. Those gorgeous dark brown eyes framed by thick lashes, held so many things in them; his emotions flashed in his eyes as much as they did across his face. When he was tense, angry or frustrated, his jaw clenched and released. When he was happy, his eyes lightened and the creases in the corners deepened. It was wholly masculine and sometimes sensual. When he was pensive or thoughtful, he rubbed the back of his neck with his hand. When he made love to her, his eyes were intense, focused, unbelievably darker and so damned sexy.

"I'm still sorry for anything that will come because of this."

His voice softened and his eyes took on that intense look as if he were memorizing her face.

"I'm not sorry at all."

He kissed her lips softly and a sound from behind her startled them both. She turned her head to see Joseph picking up the bucket he'd dropped. She smiled at Chase, "I've got to finish work here."

"I know. I've got to head back to the shop and help Gunnar and Ryder unload the signs we picked up tonight. This was just a pit stop. But a bonus that I got to see you. I didn't know you'd be working the farmers market."

She smiled. "Lily, Jan's daughter, asked me yesterday. That's why I had to work late. They were showing me all of the procedures, like which flowers to bring, where to store them, and how to cash out. I wanted to tell you I was so excited about it. It's a big deal at Forget Me Nots."

"Well, I'm glad they see the value in you, Lu. I want to see you before Saturday."

"Tomorrow?"

"It's a date."

He kissed her lightly, nodded at Joseph and walked away. Not a bad view either, his ass was amazing. She enjoyed the view for a few seconds then turned to see Joseph watching her.

His hand swept around toward the front of their tent and the table where they cashed out.

"That's why I left home to start over. Some folks will never let you forget."

22

Chase's jaw clenched and his teeth ground together. What LuAnn had done was wrong. It was criminal and Joci paid the price for a long time afterward. She still limped occasionally when the weather was damp because her hip hurt. And that bothered him. But over time he'd stayed in touch with LuAnn, visiting her in prison. She'd changed while she was there. He could see it during each visit. The hard, nasty, selfish woman had softened and a couple of times she'd told him how bad she felt. She'd found some older woman inside, Rosie, who'd taken her under her wing and counseled LuAnn. Hard to believe someone in prison for murder, or anything, would mother a troubled, young woman. Likely she'd needed to be a mother as much as LuAnn had needed one. Lord knew back in the day he'd needed Dog; the father figure who'd showed him love, respect, kindness and, most importantly, how to be a man.

Dog had tried helping LuAnn, but it was usually from afar, and for his good friend, her deceased brother, Lance.

She'd grown increasingly attached to him as she got older. He'd tried extracting himself from her especially from her inappropriate attentions. That had made her act out more to get Dog's attention; once he started seeing Joci, she treated her horribly and he only gave her negative attention. She'd told him after a while in prison that she realized his behavior toward her changed because he loved Joci.

When she'd first arrived at prison, she'd felt sorry for herself; it wasn't her fault that Joci had taken off on her bike before anyone found out she emptied the brake fluid. She'd been in denial. Then, she'd continued saying she understood that whatever her motivations were didn't matter; she was the one responsible for her actions and the consequences of them. She'd told him that she was remorseful for nearly killing Joci and the baby. That admission was what made him forgive her. She saw the wrong in what she'd done. She may not have accepted entirely the crime she'd committed, but she had started to and that was a beginning.

By her second year in prison, she'd not only softened more, she'd also matured. Rosie had begun to show her how to garden. When he'd visited her, she'd talked to him about the new flowers she'd learned to grow and how the dirt felt on her hands when she planted; she'd tell him about the smells that surrounded her in the garden and the colors so bright. He'd always had a crush on her and loved the sex. His feelings had begun to change toward her over her years in prison. He'd looked forward to his next visit before he'd even left the current one.

She'd write him letters and each one grew more positive. Granted, she'd told him she'd taken responsibility in her first year in prison, but not so much. During her second year, she'd stopped bemoaning her plight and took responsibility. She'd stopped being mad at the world and increasingly accepted the blame that was hers.

Now she was working with Greg to totally confront the crimes she'd committed and the pain she'd caused so she could move on. And she was doing well with her sessions with Greg. She didn't talk about them much, but he could see she was more peaceful. And his heart soared. She was like a caterpillar turning into a butterfly and it was remarkable. The new LuAnn had emerged a beautiful, bright, light woman with dreams and ambitions of nurturing flowers and watching them grow. She'd taken pride in making that happen; she'd transformed a simple piece of landscape at Linda's home into a piece of art alive with color and fragrance.

Working at Forget Me Nots had done wonders for her. Her employers loved her work and so did the customers. He was no expert, but the arrangements and the, what did she call them, bouquets were beautiful. Tonight, she positively beamed with pride as it appeared Gunnar and Ryder's fiancés loved her work. He loved the way her deep blue eyes became alight with hues of lighter blue. The excitement in her voice and the way her shoulders lifted and her smile, damn it lit up the room.

It pissed him off that the light had dimmed when Gunnar stared at her and started to mouth off at her. The fear on her face and the way she squared her shoulders to face what was to come was something to see. Damn, he was proud of her. She'd grown tougher, but smarter. It made his heart reach out to hers in a way he simply could not explain. Right now, he'd give it all up for her. If they gave him shit at Rolling Thunder, he'd walk away.

Just as those thoughts flowed through his brain, he had an idea. Pulling his truck to the side of the road, he grabbed the notebook he kept in the console, and a pen from inside and quickly sketched the bike he'd thought about yesterday. He'd add more detail to it later, but he was going to build this bike and name it Metamorphosis. The front would be simple but toward the back, as the eye traveled, it would be bursting with color and speed and definition. The front would be the dark blue of LuAnn's eyes, but the back, ahh, the back would be the color of her eyes when she was excited or smiling which was also the color of them when he made love to her. This would be his masterpiece. It would be a Chase Matthews Signature Collection Original and if Rolling Thunder didn't let him build it, Chief's Cycles would.

Finishing his sketch, he clipped the pen into the spiral and tucked the notebook into the console of his truck. Checking the road behind him, he pulled off the shoulder and onto the road with a new purpose and a lighter heart knowing he could forge a new path and sometimes things had to happen to force a person to that point. He'd see if he'd be traveling down a new path. Dog would be the decision maker even though he wouldn't know it. If he declined to let Chase build his own signature bike, that would be his answer.

A slow smile creased his face and he thought about LuAnn and wondered how she'd feel about living in Colorado. Other than her sister, Linda, there was nothing left for her here. Of course, she loved her job, but she could easily find another florist to work for. Actually, with the money that Gil had hinted at for him, they could afford to start their own greenhouse. She could have her own business.

It could all work.

His mind reeled with thoughts of the next step. The decisions to make. Everything except watching the road and the car that ran the stop sign.

The next thing he heard was the breaking glass as his truck spun in the road. The smell of rubber scraping on the pavement, then he was tossed about as his truck rolled into a ditch, his head hit the steering wheel and he heard nothing more.

23

Her thoughts were all over the board as she and Joseph packed up the remaining flowers, which thankfully were not abundant, and the tables, money box, water bins for the flowers, etc. What should she do? She hadn't given any real thought to where she might go if she decided to leave and start over somewhere else. And, Chase. Now that the Rolling Thunder crew would know they were together, she'd leave him with a mess and nothing to show for it.

He said he wanted her. That rocked her. He wanted her. Her. Not Olivia. One thing she knew about Chase; he'd never leave his Rolling Thunder family. Dog had been his surrogate father. She also knew she could never ask him to leave. So, her choices were to suck it up here and deal with whatever came her way or move on, alone, without Chase. The real question was, could she do that?

She loved him. She knew that now. She'd known it for a while. Sometime during her second year in prison, her thoughts and feelings for him had changed. It had been subtle, but as he visited, she asked less about Rolling

Thunder and more about Chase. What had he been doing? He'd send her letters of some of his bike drawings and she'd ask him about them. What color of a bike? Did he actually get to make it? Did it sell? How did he feel about that? She wanted to know everything about him.

Then, she'd start counting the days until she got to see him again. The women in prison were brutal bitches, too. They'd mock her and make fun of her, but she had Rosie. Rosie kept telling her to ignore the noise and focus on getting out. One day she and Rosie went out to the garden and other inmates had trampled every flower in it. She knew who they were, and her first thought was to go back inside and beat the shit out of the bitches who did it. Rosie then told her to show her strength. Her real strength, not her physical strength.

At first, she was puzzled about that. "Rosie, aren't you pissed off about this?" she asked.

"Oh, most certainly I am. But, here's the thing, LuAnn. If you don't react, they get mad. They did this to get a reaction from you. Don't react. So, let's look at what we can do."

Rosie walked to the far side of their little garden and pointed.

"We had the sunflowers here and remember us saying if we had it to do over again, we'd put them over on that side, so they didn't shade the other flowers so much. Let's do that."

Rosie picked up a couple of the trampled sunflowers and pulled the seeds from the head of them. "Let's start by gathering what we can to salvage. The flowers are trampled, but the roots aren't. We can dig them up and move them all where we want them. We can make this garden better. We can do it again. And, if we have to, we can do it again and again."

LuAnn looked Rosie in the eye, the woman had spent years inside these walls, and she was to spend many more. She'd learned the lessons. She'd seen it all.

Rosie smiled at her. "Let's go, LuAnn. We've got work to do. Grab those buckets from the garden shed so we can pull these roots up and replant."

And, that's what they did. They got to work, and they worked hard all day. By replanting, removing the trampled stems and petals that were strewn about, Rosie taught her that day how to salvage what was left of their little garden paradise and how to make it better. She'd ended that very long day with these words of wisdom to LuAnn.

"In life, things happen. Sometimes in our own control, sometimes of others' doing. We choose how to deal with it. We choose how to keep going, either with your head up and purpose in front of you or with anger and hatred. Choose wisely."

She'd lashed out in the past. She'd chosen anger and hatred in the past and now she sat behind prison walls as a result of it. Rosie was right, head up and purpose in front of her.

Remembering these words, she put her thoughts toward her purpose. What was that purpose? Without giving it a lot of thought, her purpose now was to make a living doing what she loved. Get her own place one day. Be a better person and pay it forward. And, hopefully, to develop a strong meaningful relationship with Chase. So, with that in mind, she put her thoughts toward learning as much as she could about the greenhouse and the floral business and maybe one day, she'd have a place of her own. And, she'd follow Chase's lead on how to move forward with the Rolling Thunder folks. It might be that when he had things to do with them, she'd be home working in the dirt, which had gotten her through some of her darkest days.

Climbing in the truck, Joseph climbed in the driver's seat, and they rode for the longest time in silence. Just before pulling into the parking lot of Forget Me Nots, he softly said, "You did a great job tonight. I've been coming along to help out on the farmers market nights for a little over two years now and you've sold more in one night than anyone else ever has. Good job, LuAnn."

She looked over at the kindly face of the older man. The lines and creases in the corners of his eyes a testament to the hard life he'd lived. But, he had a sparkle in those brown eyes and his face over-all was a kind one.

"What were you in prison for, Joseph?"

He took a deep breath and thought for a long time. She let the silence linger, then he softly said, "I killed a man. He tried raping my daughter and I wasn't going to make her live with that."

"Oh my God. Wasn't that self-defense?"

"No, ma'am. I killed him in his house. When he tried raping my little girl, the police let him go. No evidence. He lived just down the street from our house, and she barely could make herself leave the house she was so afraid she'd see him. I waited outside for him one night. He came home drunk. I was enraged that he could roam the streets, drunk and unafraid while my little girl was home cowering in the corner of her bedroom afraid of every noise and every minute. I followed him home, shot him, then turned myself in to the police."

"Oh, Joseph, I'm so sorry."

He turned and looked into her eyes then. "She killed herself five years later. She blamed herself for me going to prison."

Tears sprang to LuAnn's eyes and she took a deep breath to stop the sob that threatened to escape.

"I'm so sorry, Joseph. I simply can't imagine living through that."

He nodded once, parked the truck in the lot and unfastened his seatbelt.

"There are worse stories than mine and there are better stories than mine. Make yours a better story, Miss LuAnn."

$\mathcal{B}$eep. Beep. Beep. Chase's head throbbed and that damned beeping wasn't helping it. He heard soft voices. Dog. JT. They were talking about the kids, the beach where JT and Kayden had gone for their honeymoon and just small talk. But that damned beeping continued to drill into his brain.

He lifted his right hand to rub his temple but was unable to. When he couldn't lift his hand, he tugged his arm harder and felt something tighten around his wrist. Jerking repeatedly to free his arm Dog's voice came closer.

"Hey, hey, hey. Easy buddy. You're restrained because you kept yanking on your IV's and pulling them out."

His heart rate sped up as he listened to Dog's voice. "Why?"

His throat was dry, his head hurt, his mind was scrambled, and he couldn't remember why he was here. Also, where was here?

"Dry." He managed to say. His voice didn't sound like his and he felt as if he'd swallowed a five-pound bag of sand.

"You were in an accident with your truck. A drunk driver blew the stop sign and broadsided you. Your truck went careening into a ditch and rolled over a few times. You hit your head and have a concussion, some contusions, but luckily no broken bones."

"Water?" He croaked out again.

"JT just went in search of a nurse to see if we can give you water."

He nodded his head slowly. Even that hurt. He tried swallowing again which did nothing at all.

"I understand you've woken up and would like some water," a female voice said.

He tried opening his eyes, but the lights felt like a sharp, hot poker searing through his skull. He closed them and the nurse spoke again. "Maybe we should turn the lights off until he's recovered enough to stand the light."

He heard the soft click of the switch as the nurse lay her fingers on his pulse. He could hear clicking, beeping and soft noises as she checked his pulse, his heartbeat, his temperature and finally, after what seemed like an eternity, she asked, "Would you like some ice chips?"

"Yes." He managed to rasp; it simply hurt too much to nod his head.

She slowly raised the bed a couple of inches which caused him to feel dizzy, even with his eyes closed. Cracking his lids open slightly he saw only dim light coming from the window and a low task light over on the stand where the computer sat.

He felt a napkin rest against his chin, then the woman's soft voice. "I've got a few ice chips in this cup, which should help some of your thirst. I can't give you water until we know your tummy won't reject it. The last thing you want to do is vomit with a head that's been beat up."

"Yeah," he managed. He chewed the couple of ice chips

in his mouth and enjoyed the cool trickle of water as it slid down his dry throat. The stark contrast of the coolness of the melted chips against his throat which felt like it had been on fire was cooling.

Venturing another glance around the room through narrowed lids, he tried opening his eyes again. He was rather pleased for being able to open them fully this time. He saw JT grinning at him though the crease in between his eyes was deeper than normal and the stiffness of his shoulders spoke to the fact that he was worried.

He chewed a few more ice chips, then pulled his arm up again.

"Can you take this off?" he said to anyone who would listen.

"If you promise not to pull out your IV's I will."

His head barely moved, but he did his best to nod just the same. He must have gotten his message across because JT loosened the bindings on his wrists. He lifted his arms and tested the soreness in his arms and shoulders only to feel pain in every muscle. At least that's what it felt like.

"You're going to be sore for a while, Mr. Matthews. That's to be expected. I'll leave you all to visit and let the doctor know you're awake. He'll come in and talk to you to explain everything when he can."

He watched through the slits of his eyes, as he feared opening them further again might be too painful. She left the room with the whoosh of the door and Dog came to stand closer. JT scooted his chair nearer on the opposite side of the bed, and he waited as still as he could be for them to say something.

JT started, "You gave us quite a scare, buddy. You've been out of it for almost three hours."

"What day is it?"

Dog responded, "There's still an hour or so of Wednesday left."

He closed his eyes. Wednesday. Why did that seem significant?

"Where was I going?"

JT said, "You were coming back to Rolling Thunder after leaving the farmers market. You, Ryder and Gunnar went to the sign shop to pick up signs and Emma and Molly wanted to stop at the farmers market."

"Yeah." He remembered that. Then he remembered LuAnn. He'd kissed her and made a date for tomorrow. He missed her. Ryder saw them kissing and was mad. He wondered how much Dog and JT knew. It was beginning to come back to him now. Gunnar looked like he would wring LuAnn's neck and he'd stepped in and said, "Not now." Gunnar shot him an angry look. Then Ryder saw him kissing LuAnn. He knew once he got back to the shop they'd likely be ready to tell him off. Even now though, he didn't care. Not really.

"What happened?"

Dog looked down at him. "A drunk driver ran a stop sign and hit you. They've got him in custody somewhere in this hospital."

"Fucker." Chase managed to mumble.

"Yeah. Fucker." Dog repeated.

He felt so fucking tired the idea of laying back and resting took over all other thoughts. He closed his eyes and JT started saying something about the Veteran's Ride, but he didn't hear anything more.

25

_H_er heart was heavy as she quietly entered Linda and Tanner's dark house. Though it was only 10:00 o'clock, they both woke early to get to work so they usually went to bed early as well. Locking the door behind her, she took her tennis shoes off at the door, picked them up and carried them in her arm to the basement door. Silently easing herself down the basement steps, she sighed a little when she saw her bed across the room. It had truly been a long and emotional day. Relaxing her body and sleeping for a few hours sounded like a little slice of heaven.

Using the bathroom and changing into a pair of sleeping shorts and a tank top, LuAnn slid between her sheets and sighed again. Picking her phone off the table alongside her bed, she pulled up Chase's number and texted him a good night message.

"It was great seeing you tonight. Looking forward to tomorrow."

She smiled as the whoosh sounded of her message being sent, turned to the bedside table and plugged her phone in for the night. Before another thought came to her, she was fast asleep.

***

Sounds from upstairs woke her. Linda and Tanner's morning routine was now familiar and oddly comforting. She lay staring at the ceiling listening to the clinking of their forks tapping on their plates as they ate breakfast, the faint murmur of their voices as they chatted about their days. Tanner scooted his chair from the table, walked to where the coffee pot sat, walked back to Linda and likely poured her a bit of coffee to warm her half cup. She'd watched this routine dozens of times, even before she went to prison.

She rolled over to her side and checked her phone. No return message from Chase. Incredible sadness weighed on her heart as she thought about the events of last night. But, he'd said he wanted her, so she pushed the dark thoughts away, and focused on Chase's words.

With a heavy sigh, she sat up, scrubbed her hands through her hair then turned and stepped out of the bed. Stretching, she made her way to the bathroom. After brushing her teeth, running a comb through her hair and tying it up into a ponytail she exited the bathroom and pulled a clean pair of jeans from her closet. Pulling them up over her thin hips she walked to her dresser and pulled out a white t-shirt. Slipping her arms into it and then pulling her head through the neck, she pulled the bottom of the t-shirt down over her hips. Going to her closet once more she bent down and snatched up her tennis shoes, walked to her bedside table and grabbed her phone, tucking it into her back pocket then headed upstairs.

She'd not been eating breakfast lately, opting instead for a banana and then packing a lunch. Last week she'd gotten her first paycheck from Forget Me Nots and felt good about being able to help support herself a bit by contributing to the food budget and paying a small sum for rent. Linda told her she didn't have to do that, it was nice having her here, but she felt like a freeloader and wanted to pay her share. Plus, she knew Tanner and Dog were friends and Tanner had ambivalent feelings toward her and what she'd done to Joci. That made it even more necessary for her to contribute to the household.

At the top of the stairs the aroma of bacon reached her nose, and she second-guessed her breakfast decision. But, in the end stuck to her routine.

"Good morning."

Linda was first to respond, "Good morning. How did your first farmers market go?"

Pouring herself a cup of coffee, and adding a small amount of creamer, she looked over at Linda and Tanner to see their cups full. Replacing the pot on the burner she answered.

"It was pretty good. Joseph told me I sold more than anyone ever had."

"That's fantastic," Linda said.

LuAnn grabbed a banana from the bowl of fruit on the counter and sat at the table, across from Linda and at Tanner's left, with her coffee.

"It was so busy the night flew by until the last hour or so."

"I heard you saw some of the Sheppards."

Startled she stopped chewing the piece of banana and turned her head to look at Tanner. Slowly swallowing she nodded once before saying anything.

"How did you hear that?"

"I was over at Rolling Thunder helping with the stage set up and Ryder, Gunnar and Dog came back and told us what happened."

"Oh." She took a sip of coffee and her hand shook slightly. "It was a shock to all of us I think."

Tanner took a sip of coffee and nodded. "That's what Gunnar said."

Linda lay her fork and knife across her plate and stood taking hers and Tanner's plates to the sink. "Well, now that's out of the way."

Clearing her throat lightly, LuAnn said, "Not really. I saw Ryder and Gunnar and their fiancés, not Dog or Joci. They are the ones I really owe an apology to."

"Dog was there; the boys didn't tell him you were there until they were in the truck on the way back to Rolling Thunder."

"Oh." Her appetite was lost; her partially eaten banana sat on the table looking pathetic and her coffee sat cooling.

Linda came back to the table and pushed her chair in. "You should call them and ask to see them so you can apologize. Also, it will take the shock out of running into them somewhere. It's a relatively small town, you're likely to see them as you go about your day. Also, it might make things a bit easier on Chase."

Linda bent down and kissed Tanner. "Have a good day. I love you."

"I love you, too, babe." Tanner stood, then finished his coffee, put the cup in the dishwasher and stopped to look at her.

LuAnn asked, "Do you think that's what I should do? Has Dog given you any sign that he'd meet with me if I asked?"

"He hasn't indicated that or anything actually and I think we've silently agreed not to talk about you. What you did was wrong. But I do, in some ways understand that you were feeling desperate and lost. I also see that you've changed. But, they haven't seen that and don't know anything other than what you did to Joci and the aftermath of her injuries. Linda's right. Meeting with them, somewhere neutral, might at least let them know that you won't be stalking them or trying to harm them in any way."

Rubbing the space between her eyebrows, which had just begun to throb, she sighed. "I didn't know they were thinking I'd be stalking them or try to harm them."

"I don't believe that they are. But, if you were Joci, what would you think about the person who nearly killed you and your baby?"

Closing her eyes, she slowly rotated her head in circles to relieve some of the newly formed tension

"God, I hadn't thought about that. I'll try and call Dog today, if he'll accept my call."

26

Chase watched as the nurse looked at the monitors alongside his bed, wrote things on his chart, then checked his IV. The last thing she did was pull a thermometer from the little beige carry case on the tray, slide a protective sleeve on it and then looked at him. "Open your mouth, please."

He did so as he listened while the box attached to the electronic thermometer beeped, counting off the seconds as it registered his temperature. When the final beep sounded, she gently pulled the thermometer from his mouth, looked at the display and wrote his temperature down on his chart.

"Not bad for what you've been through. Slightly elevated. 101. How are you feeling today?"

"I'm feeling better than yesterday, but a bit sore everywhere."

"Well, you took quite a ride in your truck and even though you had your seatbelt on, and the air bag deployed, the pulled muscles as you rolled over and over will take a while to heal. How's your head though?"

"Not as bad as last night. The light doesn't hurt nearly as bad as it did but still seems a bit brighter than it should."

"Well, I'm sure that the reason is the concussion you suffered from all the jostling in the truck."

"Did you find my phone?"

She looked at him, her brows furrowed before she opened the top drawer on his bedside table and looked inside. Not finding his phone, she checked the second drawer and came up empty.

"Do you remember where it was when your accident occurred?"

"My pocket, I think."

The nurse turned and walked to the narrow closet across the room and opened the door. His jeans had been hung in the closet and she dug around inside his pockets until she turned with a smile. "Got it."

Bringing it to him he pushed the button only to find that the red low battery light was on.

"Shit," he muttered.

"Need a charger?"

"Yeah."

She chuckled. "We've got a drawer of them at the nurses' station. We all bring our old chargers in when we get new phones, so patients have them. If you don't mind me taking your phone, I'll run and see if I can find a charger to fit."

He handed his phone over and lay his head back and closed his eyes.

The next thing he noticed was the smell of food. Opening his eyes, his tray table had been wheeled up to him, and a fresh tray of food lay on top. His stomach roiled and he worried he'd throw up. Reaching out he pushed the tray of food away, then pulled his sheet up over his nose to mask the smell a bit.

His nurse walked in the room and looked at him. "The smell getting to you?"

"Yes."

"Can you try to eat something?

He closed his eyes and thought about eating but his stomach rebelled again.

She took his food tray and carried it from his room; to say he was grateful at that moment would be an understatement.

A few moments later she came back in and lay packets of saltine crackers, two cups of applesauce and a cup of coffee on his bedside tray.

"When you feel up to it, maybe you can nibble at these. Low odor. But, you should try to get a little something in your stomach to build your energy."

"Okay."

She then pointed to his bedside table. "I found a charger and plugged your phone in. You were fast asleep."

Slowly, he turned his head so it wouldn't throb or cause him to toss anything that had managed to stay in his stomach from last night. There lay his phone and he reached over for it. Picking it up, he pushed the button on the side that unlocked it. The bright light caused him to close his eyes a second or two before looking at his screen again.

He saw a message from LuAnn and his heart rate increased. Tapping the message, it opened, and he read her words. The last sentence, "Looking forward to tomorrow."

Shit. He didn't know how long he'd be here, but one thing was for sure, he couldn't ride today.

Starting to text her back, he'd become a bit dizzy trying to read the small text, so he'd delete it and start again. After a few tries, he typed out a message.

"I had an accident. In the hospital."

Sending that text off, he lay his phone on his lap and reached over for a packet of crackers.

His phone chimed and he excitedly picked it up to see a text from Dog.

"We got your truck and took it to the shop."

He quickly sent a thumbs up and lay his phone back down. Chewing his crackers slowly, he swallowed and waited a moment to see if his stomach would tolerate the dried food before taking another bite.

His phone chimed again, this time it was JT. "You up?"

He managed to type out, "Yeah."

Within a couple of seconds his phone rang.

"Yeah," he answered.

"Just wanted you to know that your truck is at the shop and we called your insurance agent to send an adjuster out. He'll be here later today. How are you feeling this morning?"

"Headache. My nose doesn't like the smell of food and I have to piss."

JT laughed on the other end of the line and said, "Sounds like you'll be back to normal soon. If you were ever normal that is."

"Fuck off," Chase growled.

JT laughed again. "I'll let you go piss. I just wanted you to know we're taking care of your vehicle. Don't worry about that. Get better, bro."

"Thanks."

JT hung up first and he decided he really did need to piss. Tossing the covers back, he pushed the button on his bed to raise the head allowing him to sit up. Slowly twisting so his legs dangled over the side, he waited a moment for the dizziness to subside. Once he felt ready to try, he slid off of the side of the bed until his feet touched the floor.

"Whoa, hang on, Mr. Matthews."

A nurse hastened her steps into the room. "You should have assistance the first couple of times you get up, Mr. Matthews."

"Chase. My dad was Mr. Matthews, and he was a bastard."

A cool draft reached his backside and he consciously reached back to pull his gown closed. That's when he realized, someone pulled his clothing off and he didn't remember a damned thing.

The nurse said, "Here, are you able to stand still for a minute?"

"Yeah." He was actually grateful for a minute to let his body readjust to this position.

The nurse came back with a robe and helped him into it covering his backside.

"Thanks."

"Okay, now we'll take it slow. I'm going to be right here alongside you holding your arm so I can help you if you lose your balance."

"Okay."

27

Entering the back of the greenhouse she wondered when Chase would respond. It had been a while since he told her he had been in an accident. She asked if he were alright, where he was and if there was anything she could do. It had been over an hour and he hadn't answered.

She tried focusing her mind on her work, but her worry twisted so in her gut that she thought she'd throw up. Trying to think past this moment her brain kicked into gear and she grabbed her phone and checked for a response from Chase. Still nothing.

Then she called Linda. She nervously waited for Linda to answer as she walked toward the breakroom to stash her lunch.

"What's up? Is everything okay?"

"Linda, I got a text from Chase over an hour ago that he'd been in an accident and is at the hospital. I don't know which one or how badly he's hurt. Do you think Tanner would call Dog and ask about Chase? I'm so worried about him and I want to go see him."

"Actually, I just got off the phone with Tanner and he told me Chase is at St. Catherine's Hospital. Apparently his truck rolled after he'd been hit by someone running a stop sign last night. He has a concussion, so they are keeping him for a couple of days to make sure there isn't lasting damage."

"Oh my God." She looked around worried that if she asked for time off of work this soon it wouldn't look good to her bosses. But, she also wanted to make sure Chase was alright.

"I have to go see him."

"Of course. He'd do the same for you."

"Thanks, Linda."

She ended the call and checked her messages once again. Nothing from Chase. Walking from the breakroom, she found Jan watering some of the seedlings.

"Good morning, Jan. My boy...boyfriend was in an accident and is in the hospital. I'm sorry to ask for some time off, but would you mind if I took a couple of hours to make sure he's alright?"

Jan's face crinkled in worry. "Oh honey, of course not. You go and make certain he's okay. And if you can't make it back today, just please call us and let us know, okay?"

"Thank you, Jan." Tears sprung to her eyes and she blinked rapidly to keep them from spilling down her cheeks.

"Go on now and drive carefully."

The drive to the hospital was a bit of a blur. Her mind was on Chase and how he was doing and why he hadn't responded to her. Was he in such bad shape that he couldn't even answer? Did he have to have surgery?

When she'd catch herself thinking that way, she tried to push them away and replace them with positive thoughts.

"Please be alright." She said it over and over.

Pulling to the front entrance of the hospital a valet came out to take her keys in order to park her car. She was given a number to return to the valet to retrieve her car and walked to the front desk.

"Hi. I'm looking for Chase Matthews' room."

The kindly lady behind the desk smiled. "Let me see here."

Her fingers fumbled over the keyboard and LuAnn struggled for patience.

"Ah, here he is. Room 442."

"Thank you."

Making her way to the elevators she fidgeted as she waited for an elevator to arrive. A family, laughing and giggling about a new baby, stepped out. She entered as soon as the last person got off and pushed the button for the fourth floor.

The damnable elevator stopped at each floor and her stomach felt heavier with each stop of the car.

Finally reaching the fourth floor she read the sign across from the elevator doors showing the direction for room 442. Walking down the hall she tried not looking in patients' rooms but curiosity turned her head anyway. Mostly, she wondered how serious these patients' health was so she could steel herself for what she might see when she got to Chase's room.

At the end of the hall, she saw room 442, stopped and took a deep breath. As she reached for the door handle, the door opened from inside and she jumped back. There she stood face to face with Jeremiah Sheppard.

28

Chase lay his head back onto his pillow. The nurse had given him something a while ago to ease the throbbing, but his head still hurt. Though the pounding in his head had dimmed, it was still there. His mouth had a metallic taste, and he was tired but felt fidgety and uneasy.

Raised voices from the hallway caught his attention though he couldn't make out what was being said or who it was. Then a third voice entered the argument and soon there was silence.

A nurse walked into his room. "Do you want anything to eat? I can get you a jello. You haven't eaten anything aside from crackers and applesauce."

His throat felt dry as the desert and his tongue stuck to the roof of his mouth. "Water would be good. Nothing else."

He closed his eyes as he waited on her to pour his water. The constant beeping from his heart monitor was an annoyance.

"When will they take me off this monitor? I can't stand the beeping."

The nurse clucked her tongue. "Likely today. We just needed to monitor you for a few hours to make sure you didn't go into shock."

"Shock." He mumbled.

The nurse handed him a plastic cup with cool water in it. The coolness on his fingers felt good. He lifted his head slowly, so he didn't aggravate his headache and put the cup to his lips. The cool water felt refreshing to the point that it almost burned as it slid down his throat. He could follow the path of the water all the way to his stomach.

"Not too much now, it can hurt you more than you think. Just sips at this point, please."

Pulling the cup away he reached over to set it on his tray table and noticed that his hand trembled slightly.

"I hope that'll go away."

The nurse walked over and followed his gaze. "Trauma. You've been through a lot and this is one of the ways your body releases it. I haven't known many who have had lasting effects of tremor in your condition. But you should bring it up with your doctor when you see him. He should be around shortly. Anything else I can get you?"

Slowly shaking his head, he lay back and closed his eyes. He hoped LuAnn would be here soon. He needed to see her.

Deep in his subconscious he heard a door open. It was quiet, but yet a sound he could recognize. Quiet footsteps came closer to him and he imagined an aftershave similar to his own.

"I see you're still laying around napping."

He opened his eyes to see JT smiling down at him.

"Fuck off." He teased back.

"Are you feeling better today?"

"Yeah, some. Head still throbs like a bitch, would love for that to go away."

JT sat in the chair alongside his bed. "You hit your head pretty good." He was quiet for a moment then said. "I saw your notebook. I like the drawings of the bike. Sexy."

Chase studied his friend for a long time to see if he was serious or giving him shit.

"Thanks. I'm going to build it."

JT nodded. "I showed Dad. He liked it, too, but said it strayed too much from the usual Rolling Thunder bikes. He said it was too provocative and he wasn't sure he'd stand behind it. It took him a long time to accept my bikes, too. But, you and I can build it in your garage. Once he sees it, maybe he'll change his mind. "

Disappointment sat heavy in his chest. That was what he'd feared would happen; somehow he knew it deep in his bones. Recalling the many times JT and Dog had argued over JT wanting to build the bikes he dreamed of and Dog's resistance to his design made his heart feel heavier than ever. Dog was a great businessman, but he didn't embrace change or new bike ideas easily unless JT as Head Designer and his son pitched them and took most of the credit despite both of them designing the bikes. Chase had a tough decision to make now.

The door opened and Chase twisted his head. A cleaning woman came in and lay towels on the dresser across the room. Only nodding once and quietly leaving, Chase sank down into the mattress in disappointment. Seemed as though that was the theme today.

"Who did you expect to see or don't I want to know."

Looking his friend in the eyes Chase pushed the button on his bed and slowly raised his head up to more of a sitting position, pleased that it didn't cause the pain to shoot through his temples.

"I thought LuAnn would be here by now. Sorry if you didn't want to know, but you asked."

Clearing his throat, JT sat forward, his elbows on his knees and stared directly into Chase's eyes.

"She was here earlier, but Dad told her to go away and not come back."

Tears sprang to his eyes and he sniffed as his nose started running. It was the instant pang of hurt that hit him hard.

"He had no business to tell her to go away. It's my business. She is my business. Not yours. Not his. Not Ryder's. Not Gunnar's. Mine."

"Look Chase, you know what's she's done..."

"Yes, I do. And, for the record, no one could be sorrier than she is. But, of course none of you will ever give her the chance to prove..."

The door opened and Dog stepped in. "I didn't hear an apology from her."

"Did you give her the chance, or did you just butt in where you don't belong and tell her to leave without so much as asking me if I wanted her here?"

Dog straightened his shoulders, his eyes darted to JT's then back to his.

"What do you see in her? Doesn't it matter to you that she almost killed Joci and Maddy?"

"I can't explain what I see in her, all I know is that I love her. Of course, it matters what almost happened to Joci and Maddy. But, for the record, and I know it's like splitting hairs, she never meant for anyone to get hurt. She thought someone would see the brake fluid on the floor and have to refix the bike. An inconvenience. She also knows how stupid, destructive and immature that was. And, she's paid the price."

Dog scraped his hand down his face, frustration and exasperation was clear from his expression.

A long silence fell in the room and Chase's heartbeat raced as he wondered what his next move would be.

Dog turned to leave but stopped. "For the record, I will never forget what LuAnn did to my family despite all the help and bullshit I'd gone through with her over the years. Granted, I did it out of respect for Lance, but I still did it. I never begrudged her anything she had. And, all her bad decisions were of her own doing, not anyone else's. That said, you have to make your own decisions and whether this one is a bad one or a good one, will only be determined by you."

"LuAnn knows you'll never forget. She won't either. But, haven't you always said we need to forgive or the hate in our hearts will eat away at us?"

Without another word, Dog left the room. He lay his head back on the pillow and took in a deep shaky breath. JT broke the silence.

"I'll tell you this, Chase. When I met Kayden, things were rocky at first, but once I knew I loved her, no one would change my mind. So, I get it, your heart wants what it wants, and I hope, for your sake, LuAnn makes you happy. But, you must know she'll never be accepted at Rolling Thunder."

"I'm aware."

JT stood with a heavy sigh. "I'll see you later man. Hope you feel better soon."

JT walked through the door and the first thing Chase did was reach for his phone and look through his texts. That's when he saw several texts from LuAnn asking where he was. He'd never answered and now his brain was confused at how she knew where he was.

With shaking fingers, he sent out a text to LuAnn.

29

*L*uAnn's phone chimed a text and she quickly pulled it from her back pocket. Her heart hammered in her chest when she saw the message from Chase.

"I'm so sorry Dog gave you a hard time this morning. I had no idea you were out there. Please come back, he's gone, and I don't expect to see him here again."

Her fingers shook with excitement and also worry. What had he done?

"I can come after work. About two hours."

"I'll watch the clock."

She smiled, held her phone close to her chest for a moment and inhaled deeply. Lily walked into the greenhouse and LuAnn quickly tucked her phone in her back pocket, and her cheeks burned with embarrassment at being caught on her phone. Again.

"Is your man doing alright?"

Your man. Wow, that sounded...nice.

"Yes, he asked when I could come back to see him. I told him only two hours." Her smile broadened.

"I'm happy to hear he's doing well." Lily continued on through this greenhouse into the back greenhouse. Forget Me Nots consisted of the front store then the four separate greenhouses. Each had its own purpose and grew different varieties of plants and flowers. She was happy she mostly worked with the flowers, but she also had some days where they took care of the vegetables and she'd been learning more and more about them as well. The job was incredibly interesting.

Setting her mind to the task before her, she began working the nutrients into the soil with her hands. The feel of the cool soil and the aroma of the fragrant nutrients also made her smile. She was helping life to grow here. Beauty. The colorful flowers and their individual aromas made for such a happy place. It was healing to the soul. At least hers.

"LuAnn, Mrs. Smythe is here for her arrangement." Jan called from the back of the store.

Looking up, she nodded, reached for a rag to wipe her hands and began walking to the store. A little nervous would be an apt description of her feelings. She'd impressed Mrs. Smythe with the floral choices from the catalogue, but now she'd know for sure if her choices were perfect. This felt like a big deal. Lily said Mrs. Smythe was a very good customer; it wouldn't do to not please her.

Entering the back of the store she walked to the floral cooler where the arrangements were kept after they were made. The blue speckled coffee pot and the purple and green arrangement looked fantastic together.

Pulling the unique arrangement from the cooler, she turned to walk to the front of the store. The overly large arrangement was heavy and would certainly make a stunning centerpiece. Entering the front of the store she set the heavy container on the counter and looked around for

Mrs. Smythe. Seeing her across the store looking at candle holders, LuAnn walked around the counter to get Mrs. Smythe's attention. The handsome woman turned around, her sharp blue eyes first landing on LuAnn then switching over to the arrangement on the counter.

"Oh, my word, that is the most stunning arrangement I've ever seen."

She walked past LuAnn to the counter and stood in amazement before the flowers. LuAnn smiled as she followed Mrs. Smythe; she was clearly happy with her choices. A sigh of relief released LuAnn's shoulders and the tightness in her back a bit.

Walking behind the counter she smiled as she watched Mrs. Smythe turn the arrangement back and forth to see the whole thing.

"LuAnn, I am absolutely in love with this."

"I'm happy and relieved to hear that. I'm extremely proud of it myself to be honest with you."

"You should be. I am going to be the envy of my Bridge Club and I have you to thank for it. I'm so excited I could burst."

LuAnn laughed. It felt good to be appreciated for doing something good. Something she loved at that. This was the feeling she'd always been missing. Feeling as if she was wanted because she did a good job was wonderful. How immature she'd been before. It was embarrassing to think of it now.

Pushing her old inferior thoughts away, she rang up Mrs. Smythe's purchase. "I can carry it to the car for you, it's heavy."

"Oh, thank you, dear, I appreciate it."

LuAnn pulled a large cardboard box from under the table behind her, set the arrangement in the box and wrapped the whole thing with a clear plastic bag. "This will protect it until you get home. Once you get it on the table where it will sit, take a spray bottle and give the whole arrangement a light mist with water."

"I'll do just that. Thank you."

LuAnn followed Mrs. Smythe out the door of the store, her heavy burden tucked tight to her body to keep from dropping it.

She set it on the floor of the backseat passenger side of the car, tucked some newspaper around the outside of the box to keep it upright and then smiled her brightest smile to Mrs. Smythe.

"Have a great dinner. I can't wait to hear how the ladies are green with envy."

"Oh, I'll certainly let you know."

LuAnn watched Mrs. Smythe drive away from the store, her mood lifted once again and more eager than ever to see Chase and tell him about her day. At least her afternoon, the morning hadn't been all that great.

She walked back to the greenhouse to find Jan and Lily waiting for her. She stopped short worried she'd done something wrong.

Lily was the first to comment. "LuAnn, you did a fantastic job on that arrangement. Mom and I think your reward should be to see your man early. With pay. Please go enjoy his company and make him feel better."

Her eyes teared up. "Oh, wow, thank you so much. You don't know how much that means to me."

Jan replied. "It's our pleasure. Thank you for doing such a great job."

As she drove to the hospital, LuAnn decided to send pictures of her arrangement to Rosie. Hopefully, she'd appreciate how her student had excelled. At least in this area of her life.

30

Chase looked at the time on his phone. Another hour and fifteen minutes. He couldn't wait to see her.

His thoughts went to the one thing he'd never said out loud to anyone. "I love her." He loved LuAnn. He'd actually been in love with her for years, even though he'd never told her so. His love grew for her as she matured in prison. Her metamorphoses. He knew that people just didn't change all of their bad behaviors, but actually, one of LuAnn's worst behaviors was trying to get Dog's attention. She'd likely not be doing that anymore. She'd changed how she dressed, and he liked this LuAnn so much better. She was sexy, always had been, but that hard edge and trashy component that his younger self liked was now gone. In many ways, he'd matured while LuAnn was in prison, too.

The door to his room opened and he casually glanced over. Surprised was such an inept word for seeing LuAnn walk through his door early.

She quickly walked to him and he reached his hand out to touch her.

"Oh my God. Are you in pain? Are you hurt anywhere else besides your head? Can I hug you?"

His voice cracked with emotion when he said, "Yes."

She tentatively leaned down to hug him, and he pulled her right onto the bed with him. He didn't care if she hit sore spots, he needed to hold her. To feel her against him.

He wrapped his arms around her tiny body and let the tears that flooded his eyes fall down his temples and wet his pillow. Her body shook as her tears spilled and they both lay still, their arms wrapped as tightly as they could be for a long time. This was more healing than anything the doctors could do for him.

LuAnn lifted her head and swiped the tears from her eyes. She scooted to his side and he moved over to allow her some room.

"Tell me true. Where are you hurt?"

Those blue eyes of hers bore into his dark brown ones and he thought he'd just lay here and look into them for a long time. But, when he didn't answer she raised her eyebrows expecting an answer.

"I have a concussion, which is the only reason they're keeping me here a few days. Otherwise, I have bumps and bruises everywhere it seems. I had my seatbelt on, but I still flopped around a bit and mostly, it's where my seatbelt held me in place and the air bag deployed."

She looked down to his chest, lifted the hospital gown away from his neck and peeked inside.

"Oh my God, Chase. You're purple." She moved to get up, but he held her there.

"Please just lay here with me a bit."

"I don't want to hurt you."

"You won't. You aren't."

She stared into his eyes; her left hand cupped his jaw while her thumb softly floated over his lips.

"I've been so worried about you."

"I know and thanks." He took in a deep breath. "I'm so sorry Dog chewed you out this morning. He had no right and I've told him so."

"Chase, don't get fired over me. We'll figure a way around all of this. I understand I'm not welcome at their events. I get it."

"I won't get fired. He stepped in to help out and I'm very grateful. He took care of getting my truck to the shop. He also had the insurance adjuster go to Rolling Thunder to look it over and I'm grateful for that, too. But, it's different when it comes to my personal life. Who I date. Who I'm with. Who I..." Hesitating, he swallowed. "Who I love that is none of his business."

Her eyes rounded. "You love me?"

He chuckled because, seriously, how could she not see it. "Yes."

"Oh God. Chase. I love you, too."

Her lips touched his. It was soft, sweet and so momentous. His right hand cupped the back of her head and held her there so the kiss would last.

When he let go of her, she lifted her head slightly. "It feels so good to say it to you. I never wanted to scare you away."

He laughed, then coughed, then winced. "My God, LuAnn, if I didn't get scared away after all you've done, what made you think telling me you loved me was going to scare me away?"

She giggled. "Sometimes it's the smallest thing that scares a person, not the big things."

"True that."

The door opened and a nurse walked in. "Well now, it looks like you're feeling much better."

He chuckled again. "Now that my girl is here, nothing

can stop me. I have a goal to get sprung from this place as soon as possible."

"The doctor is on his way in and you can talk to him about that and the trembling in your hands you were concerned about. LuAnn gently sat up, and then stood so the nurse could check his vitals. She walked to the other side of the bed and sat in the chair watching him as the nurse took his temperature and checked his pulse.

"I need you to slip your arms out of your gown, Mr. Matthews so the doctor can look at your bruises. I'm afraid you'll have to step outside, miss."

"LuAnn can stay with me while the doctor does his examination."

He struggled a bit and LuAnn quickly got up to help him. When his chest was exposed, tears welled in her eyes and her fingers gently brushed his bruised ribs and left shoulder.

"It's okay, Lu. Nothing's broken, the bruises will go away."

She nodded but didn't say anything. Within a few seconds the door opened again and a man with dark hair and a darker olive complexion walked in.

"Hello, I'm Doctor Epps."

"Hi, Doc. Chase Matthews and my girlfriend, LuAnn Mason."

Doctor Epps looked over at LuAnn and nodded, "Nice to meet you both."

He pulled the chart from the foot of the bed, looked it over, and then neared the bedside. He examined the bruises running down and across Chase's chest and then his left arm. Dr. Epps gently touched and added pressure to his left shoulder, and then his ribs; Chase managed not to groan too loudly but damn that did hurt. Pulling the pen light from the front pocket of his lab coat, Dr. Epps then shined the light into Chase's eyes, moved it around watching his pupils dilate a few times then clipped the pen light back into his pocket.

"How is your headache?"

"It's dulled quite a bit through the day."

"Good." Doctor Epps wrote something on his chart then looked at him. "I think we can let you go home tomorrow. The nurse mentioned that you were worried about trembling in your hands. I wouldn't be concerned unless it persists for more than a week or so. If it does continue past that time, schedule an appointment with your doctor. Remember you had quite an accident. Do you have someone at home to help you out if you become ill? Moving around might be difficult the next couple of days and it would help if someone were there to help you manage."

He turned his head to LuAnn, "Can you stay with me and play nurse?"

Her cheeks burned bright red, but her lips curved up into a beautiful smile. "I can stay and help you out. Not sure how great a nurse I am, but I can cook and clean and help with chores."

He smiled at her. It would be nice having her there with him. Turning to Doctor Epps, he replied, "Yep, I have help."

The doctor chuckled and so did the nurse. "Okay. I'll be around in the morning to sign your discharge papers."

31

As the doctor and nurse left the room, LuAnn sat on the side of Chase's bed. "I honestly don't know how good a nurse I'll be, but I do promise to try my hardest to help you out. For the time being, do you need groceries at home? I can get some shopping done and put something in the crock pot so you can have a nice lunch when we get you home tomorrow."

His smile, oh how she loved his smile. When he turned it toward her it felt like a spotlight shining right on her.

"I haven't had the time to get groceries and the cupboards are bare I'm afraid."

She smiled right back at him, it was hard not to because despite the circumstances right now, she was stupidly happy. He loved her. She loved him. They could do this.

"I'll go to the grocery store when I leave here. Tell me some of your favorites and I'll make sure I pick them up."

Pulling her phone from her back pocket, she opened a shopping list app she had and turned on the microphone. As Chase listed his favorites, the app wrote them out.

"Chocolate ice cream. Not with marshmallows - just

good old chocolate ice cream. Spinach for a great salad. Bacon, eggs, milk, cheese. You'll need to check the freezer to see what I have in there for meat. An old-fashioned roast beef with potatoes and carrots sounds like a slice of heaven right now. Oh, and beer and bottled water. I like smoked almonds for a snack and..."

She laughed. "I think you're hungry."

"I am. I didn't eat much yesterday and I wasn't hungry this morning, but now, I want to eat everything in sight."

He tugged her hand pulling her close and his lips captured hers. His hands framed her face as his lips alternated between soft kisses then consuming long, wet hungry kisses and it was hard to tell which she liked more. Matching his kisses with hers she planted her hands on either side of his hips, so she didn't push against his bruises and allowed him to kiss her all he wanted because she wanted all of his kisses.

"Well, it looks like you're being taken care of."

Her heart skipped a beat as Gunnar's voice ripped through the air. She sat back, but Chase held her hand, keeping her on the side of the bed with him.

"I'm in good hands." He smiled at her as he answered Gunnar.

Gunnar's eyes slid over to hers and her skin crawled at the venomous look in his.

"I hope that's right, Chase."

Chase's hand squeezed hers while he responded to Gunnar. "I am. How are things at the shop? I think it's safe to say I won't be much help to you for the Veteran's Ride. I'm sorry for that."

"We're sorry, too. I just wanted to pop in and see how you're doing. Dad said you had words today. For the record, he feels bad about it."

Gunnar's handsome blue eyes once again landed on

hers and almost as if daring her to say something. He waited. Her breathing hitched up a notch and she wasn't sure if he was daring her to fight with him or testing her resolve. What she knew is that Chase cared for Gunnar and she loved Chase. While Gunnar would never give her the time of day again, she hoped at least they could be in the same room without fighting. If she had to sit and take his shit, she'd do it. Just like when she was in prison, she'd learned to sit and take the insults and vile words tossed her way from the other inmates trying to start a fight with her. At first she'd bitch back, but after two visits to the infirmary for cuts and bruises, she learned to sit and take it. She looked at it as her punishment for all she'd done. At least here in the outside world, she could walk away if she wanted to.

Focusing on Chase's hand holding hers, she simply stared back at Gunnar, keeping her face as neutral as she could. She wouldn't cower down.

"I feel bad about it, too. But, like it or not, I'm with LuAnn. I love her and she loves me. That is no one else's business but ours."

Gunnar nodded. "I'll take off then, I just wanted you to know we're thinking of you. Hope you'll be well enough to come to the wedding next Saturday."

Gunnar slowly turned without another word and stepped out the door. The room was silent for a few moments and she felt bad for Chase. This was Rolling Thunder's big weekend of the year and he was going to miss it. And his co-workers and family at Rolling Thunder.

"You know, we can get in my car and drive to somewhere along the ride and watch them all go by on Saturday. I'll pack a picnic for us."

His eyes turned to hers and his lips curved up into a soft smile. "We'll see about that on Saturday morning."

"Okay." Taking a deep breath, she asked one more question. "Who's getting married next Saturday?"

He adjusted himself in bed. "Gunnar and Emma and Ryder and Molly. They're having a double wedding. It's long overdue, they were supposed to get married a couple of years ago, but then Emma got pregnant and they all decided to wait until after the baby was born, then Molly had to sit through another trial with her stepfather after he kidnapped her, and they didn't want to plan a wedding during that time and so now they're finally getting around to making it all official. Not that it's stopped them from living as if they are already married."

"Wow, that's a lot of stuff to deal with. Glad they're finally getting their wedding. Emma and Molly seemed excited about the flowers when I saw them last night at the farmers market."

"Yeah." He pulled the blanket back and struggled to turn in the bed. "Your nursing duties start now, Lu. I've got to go to the bathroom, and I can't walk on my own yet."

32

Chase wrapped his arm around LuAnn's shoulders and gingerly took small steps until they reached the kitchen entrance from the garage. There were only two steps he had to climb, but he hadn't tried to climb steps since his accident. LuAnn stepped up first and waited on the first step for him to climb up. It wasn't as hard as he'd imagined it would be. Once he was steady on his feet, she opened the door, took the second step, and they repeated their maneuvers.

Inside the kitchen, the aromas that he inhaled made his stomach growl.

"Damn girl that smells fantastic."

She giggled. "You said you wanted roast beef, potatoes and carrots. That's what you're getting."

"Damn."

"Sofa or table?"

"Neither. Recliner, please."

Slowly, they made their way through the savory kitchen and to the living room. LuAnn stopped before the recliner and he removed his arm from her shoulders but then kissed the top of her head.

"What do you need me to do to help you sit down?"

Taking little steps, he maneuvered himself, so he was standing in front of the recliner. "I think I can do this part." He tried lowering himself slowly, but a sharp pain shot across his ribs and he landed with a thud followed by a howl as his ribs punished him for the wrong move.

"Chase? Oh my God, are you alright?"

She knelt in front of him. At the moment, he could only see a blur as his eyes failed to focus. Taking shallow breaths, he closed his eyes laying a hand on her right shoulder, so he had contact with her. After a few moments he managed to open his eyes.

"The sofa would likely have been better, but then again, I'm not sure. So, if you don't mind, I'm going to take a little rest because that excursion just wore me out."

"Of course." She stood, pulled a blanket from the back of the sofa and lay it over his lap, then she gently kissed his lips. "Would you like water, juice or milk?"

"I don't have..."

"I shopped last night. You've got a fully stocked fridge and pantry."

"Lu." He grabbed her hand and kissed her fingers. "Thank you."

She giggled. "That's Nurse Lu to you. Take a nap, I'll wake you when lunch is ready."

She walked back to the kitchen and he dozed off listening to her humming, smelling a delicious lunch and happy to be home.

His phone ringing woke him up. As he realized what he was hearing he dug into his pocket and pulled his phone out.

"Yeah. Chase here."

He heard laughing on the other end of the line. "Sounds like maybe I woke you. This is Gil Jones from Chief's in Colorado."

"Hi Gil. Yeah, you caught me napping. I was in an accident a couple of days ago and I'm now home convalescing."

"Well, shit son, I'm sorry to hear that. Are you going to be alright?"

"Yeah, just a few more days and I'll be fine. Mostly got my bell rung and my air bag and seatbelt did a number on my rib cage."

"Well, I am sorry to hear that. But, I'll send up some good prayers for you to heal quickly."

Chase chuckled. "Thanks. I'll take them."

"So, I'm just checking in with you on our discussion earlier this week. Have you given any thought at all to my offer?"

"I have actually. But first, hang on Gil." He pulled his phone away from his ear and scrolled through his pictures. Finding the picture of the bike he'd drawn just before his accident, he texted that to Gil. "I just texted you a picture of a drawing I made just before my accident. Take a look and give me your honest opinion on that."

He listened as he could hear Gil on the other end, but he looked around wondering where LuAnn was.

"Hot damn, Chase, that there is a sexy-ass bike. Did you make it yet?"

"No. I want to. If we can make this work, it'll be the first Chase Matthews design for Chief's Cycles."

Gil whistled on the other end of the phone but said nothing for a long time.

"What do we have to work out, Chase?"

"Okay, can you give me a little time here? I need to talk to my girl. If I can find her, I'm not sure where she's at right now. I want to have this conversation with her and see what she thinks. Then I think we need to come out for a face to face."

"Them's the best words I've heard all day, Chase. Give me a call tomorrow and let's nail down some of the details. I'm looking forward to seeing you in person."

"Sounds good. I'm looking forward to seeing you in person as well, I just need a little time."

He ended the call and scooted to the edge of his recliner. Using his leg muscles, he managed to stand without the stabbing pain in his ribs. Turning toward the kitchen, he saw LuAnn standing there, fresh from outside, a look of fear on her face.

"Who are you excited to see in person?"

Her gorgeous blue eyes welled with tears as he made his way slowly to her. Once he was standing before her, he pulled her close and wrapped his arms around her, enjoying the way her body felt against his.

"We need to talk."

33

Staring across the corner of the table at Chase, she could see the indecision in his eyes. His gorgeous dark brown, earnest eyes. "So, you actually are thinking about leaving Rolling Thunder?"

"I am."

His hand reached out and took hers, their fingers laced together, and he squeezed.

"But you love them. Dog took you in as one of his own."

"I do and he did. But, sometimes families find themselves moving away from each other. Dog won't let me build this bike."

He pointed to his phone of the spectacular bike drawing he'd shown her. "As I recall, JT had to fight like a beast to let Dog allow him to build his bikes. Dog is great. He's a great businessman, but he's reluctant to stray too far from the path that has built his business. I understand that, I do. But, I'm ready to stray outside the lines a bit. Gil will allow me that freedom."

Her stomach twisted. This was so out of the blue from any conversation she thought they'd be having today.

"Wow. I don't even know what to say."

"I want you to come with me. Fresh start. For both of us. They aren't going to welcome you into their circle, Lu."

Turning her head to stare out the patio doors a sadness settled in her heart. "Chase, you can't make this big of a decision for me. The implications are long lasting."

"Fuck, Lu, I thought you'd be jumping for joy."

He stood slowly pain evident on his beautiful face.

"I'm doing this for myself as much as for you. It's not something I was thinking about before Gil called. And, actually, when he called me I told him no. But the seed was planted, and now things are pointing to the fact that maybe it is meant to be this way."

She looked into his eyes, trying to discern his level of sincerity. He seemed completely serious.

"Lu, let's at least fly out there and look at the place. We can see if the area offers some of the other things we'd want in life. If nothing else, we'll get a vacation out of it, some time together, just the two of us."

"I'll have to see what I can work out at Forget Me Nots. They've been good to me."

She stood facing him, and when he held his arms open, she willingly walked into them. The warmth and security she felt wrapped in his arms, his steady heartbeat at her ear, the solidness of his body against hers it was where she always wanted to be.

"Let's do this. Let's eat, I'm famished. Then see what you can do about getting some time off at work. We'll chat about it again once you know something."

"Sounds good." She mumbled into his chest.

Loosening her arms around him, she stepped back, "You need help sitting down?"

"No, I need to do this on my own."

Stepping back, she watched as he sat in the chair,

without much of a problem, just one small grimace. Turning to the cupboard, she took out plates, silverware and napkins and lay them on the table. Busying herself with the pot roast and arranging the potatoes and carrots on the plate she allowed her mind to wonder about a change as big as this. Joseph had managed and he didn't have anyone with him; he just did it on his own.

Carrying the meal, which smelled fantastic if she did say so herself, to the table, she set it down, went to the refrigerator to get them each a bottle of water and sat to Chase's left. Before they could begin eating, his phone chimed a text and he glanced down at it and smiled.

"Greg is on his way over. Do we have enough for one more?"

"Of course, we do." She began adding another place setting to the table and thought he was the perfect person for them to talk to about this big move and all the motives behind it.

The doorbell rang and she walked through the living room to the front door. Greg's smiling face greeted her when she opened the door, and it was impossible not to smile in return.

"Come in, it's so good to see you."

"Good to see you, too. Are you a nurse now?"

Laughing she shook her head. "Hardly. But I did cook a mean pot roast if you're so inclined."

"Sadly, I'm always hungry."

"Chase is at the table, please come on in."

Greg walked toward Chase and LuAnn closed the door behind him. Following his path to the dining area, she offered him a drink and he replied. "Water, please, the same as you two."

After handing him his water, she resumed her seat and began eating as Chase and Greg chatted about his accident and his injuries. The transformation in Chase's posture improved just seeing Greg. She wondered at the miracle of having people you loved and respected in your life and how that reformed even the smallest of things. Attitude was everything.

Her mind continued to wander as she half listened. One thing that struck her hardest was that she and Linda, while they'd always gotten along so well, never really had conversations like Chase and Greg were having now. They chatted about the weather, how she was doing, but never in depth, it was more superficial. It had always been that way though. Sometimes families were incredibly close like Ryder, JT and Gunnar and others weren't. She loved Linda, but in the whole scheme of things they weren't that close. They didn't shop or spend time doing other things together. Thinking on it now, it was a sobering feeling.

"LuAnn?"

She looked up to see both Greg and Chase staring at her. "I'm sorry, my mind wandered, what were you saying?"

Greg chuckled, "I asked you your thoughts on Chase's proposal to move to Colorado."

"Oh. Sorry. I'm curious about seeing it. I'm interested in what Chase thinks of it. And it sounds like an amazing opportunity for him to broaden his design career and really come into his own without being in JT's shadow."

"Okay... That sounds like the perfect answer someone would want to hear but your tone isn't convincing."

She looked over to Chase and his expression was a mixture of interest and dread. Turning back to Greg, she continued, "I wish I knew how much Chase wants for himself and how much for me. Because..." Glancing at Chase again, she took his hand in hers. "It has to be for you, Chase. You can't turn away from everyone you love here for me. You have to feel it in there ..." she pointed to his heart, "for it to work."

"I do feel it in here." He lay his hand over his heart. "For me and for you. And, I don't think it's bad for me to also want this for you and for us."

Greg then looked at her and asked, "What do you want, LuAnn?"

34

Chase awoke to LuAnn's voice in the other room. Stretching his sore, tired muscles he worked himself up to a sitting position, rather pleased that he could do that much by himself. Progress.

"I appreciate that, thank you. Yes, I certainly will."

Cupboards opened and closed, and his curiosity got the best of him. Their conversation with Greg had been enlightening last night and as a true friend does, he encouraged them both to follow their hearts, even if it meant they'd leave the area, he'd always be there for them.

With a slight grunt, he stood, snagged a clean t-shirt from his top drawer and slipped it over his head as he ambled out of the bedroom and toward the kitchen. His bare feet were silent on the carpeting as he approached the bright dining area, which was just in front of the kitchen. LuAnn stood staring out of the patio doors leading to the backyard, her arms hugging her waist as if she were protecting herself from hurt.

His stomach plummeted as he watched her body,

standing so still, contemplating something that seemed like a heavy burden.

"Hey."

She turned at the sound of his voice and her arms unwrapped, and she tucked her fingers into her front pockets.

"Hey."

"What's up?"

She lightly cleared her throat. "I just called Linda this morning to tell her about Colorado. She said it sounded like a great opportunity for you."

He grew wary as he stepped closer to her.

"It is a great opportunity."

"Yeah."

"And?"

"That was it. No, I'll miss you. Oh, you're just getting yourself together, nothing." She walked to the coffee pot and poured two cups. "I'd been thinking last night that I love her, and I know she loves me, but we aren't really close."

She handed him a cup of the steaming, aromatic, brew then turned and opened the oven where the amazing smell of her egg bake filled the room. Turning it in the oven, she closed the door and turned back to him.

"It's kind of sad really. But you know I've never made any real close friends. Last night when Greg came, your shoulders straightened, your mood lifted, and I could see your whole demeanor was changed by having Greg here to talk to. You've made that wonderful connection with him and the Rolling Thunder guys, and I guess, I've never really done that. So, I suppose I'm just having many self-doubts and wondering if something is wrong with me that I don't have that connection with anyone and never have."

"You have me. You make me feel like I can change the world."

His heart hurt for her. She was right though she hadn't made that amazing connection with anyone. A friend. Someone of the same sex who she could shop with, have fun with, enjoy time with.

A sad smile formed on her pretty face. "And I am eternally grateful for you. And, I love you so much. But, I don't have girlfriends. Or even, a girlfriend to have coffee with or a shopping day."

"Don't you think a lot of that is because you've always been focused on yourself or getting Dog's attention? And, I'm not trying to cause trouble, but you've never really put yourself out there as someone who gave a shit about anyone else."

He watched her swallow a big lump in her throat and her eyes welled with tears. Sniffing she angrily swiped at her eyes. "You're one hundred percent right. How is it that you love me then?"

He set his cup on the table and closed the distance between them.

"I love you because I do. I see in you the person I used to be so many years ago. Lost. Afraid. Alone. All of that makes my heart want to be connected to yours. The fact that your past has kept you from making lasting relationships is who you were. This person right here before me now, who has learned some incredibly hard lessons, and has been working on herself, just had a realization that life can be different. You've been working on becoming the new you since prison and more so with your counselling sessions with Greg. You've started to make friends with your co-workers at Forget Me Nots. And those are the things that make me love you more. You're still doing the hard work. Admitting weaknesses and faults is the hard work. You think I haven't done that in the past? Shit, Lu, the whole time you were in prison I was doing all my hard work. It's what led me to Greg and his church. It's what led me back to you when I would have walked away that first year. It's what propels me forward now to do what's good for me. And for you."

Her arms wrapped around him and she cried softly into his t-shirt. He kept his left arm wrapped around her waist as his right hand came up and cupped her head to his chest. His heartbeat increased and for the first time since she'd come home from prison and they'd gotten together, he felt, deep in his bones, that they were going to make it and would always be stronger together. It was a bonus that his body responded to this moment, too. He'd been worried when he hadn't had an erection since his accident. He was healing and getting back in the game. His left hand slid down her back and to her ass, pulling her body into his.

She froze for a split second, then moved her hips back and forth against his thickening penis and his breathing hitched.

Her hands slid down his ass and realizing he was only wearing underwear, she smiled, slid her thumbs into his briefs and pulled them down as far as she could reach. This morning was definitely looking up.

35

It had been a couple of weeks since they'd had sex. The week prior since he'd been working at Rolling Thunder to get ready for the ride, she'd thought of him several times and 'helped herself' more than once as images of him filled her mind. She wasn't sorry.

As her hands pulled his briefs down around his fine ass, his skin heated, and the firmness of his ass felt wonderful against her fingertips. Flattening her hands on his ass, she enjoyed the feel of him.

His lips sought hers and her fingers floated around his hips and found his erect full penis straining forward. Her right hand wrapped around his girth, the softness of the skin such contrast to the ruggedness of the man. When her thumb floated over the tip, it jerked in her hand and precum formed at the tip. Swirling her thumb through its wetness, she covered the head of his penis in his precum and pumped his length with her other hand. Finding his balls, tightening in her hands, the course hairs and smoothness of his skin opposites, was thrilling to her.

Pulling a fraction from his lips she mumbled, "Let's go to bed so you're comfortable."

"Comfortable isn't what I want right now, Lu."

She giggled against his lips. "By comfortable I meant, you can lay there while I ride you."

"That's what I want."

Chase began walking backwards and she followed him closely, never moving her hands away from him, their lips continuing to test and taste each other. Once they reached the bedroom door, his hands slid to her ass, then came back up and cupped her breasts. Pinching her nipples until they puckered, and she let out a groan. He sat slowly on the edge of the bed and she pulled away long enough to finish pulling his briefs down his legs. On her way back up, she licked her way up his cock and quickly sucked him into her mouth.

The groan that sounded from deep in his chest told her everything she needed to know. She pulled up then sucked her way back down to the base of his cock and he slowly laid back on the bed, his breath coming in sharp pants. His balls drew up tight to his body and she was sad it would be over soon. Stopping she stood up, pulled her t-shirt and bra off and let them fall to the floor. His eyes roved over her body and it was almost as if she could feel him touching her the way he looked at her.

Unzipping her jeans, she shimmied them over her hips, giving him a bit of a show, her breasts swaying with the movement. She did the same thing with her panties and on her way back up, she fondled a breast in each hand. He growled and she loved it.

Smiling she slowly climbed up on the bed and straddled his body eager to feel him inside of her once again. She was wet, so sliding down onto his cock was easy and watching his eyes roll to the back of his head made it all worth it. She enjoyed rocking his world. She enjoyed it a lot.

Leaning forward, she captured his lips with hers, sliding her tongue inside his mouth and tasting him completely. His hands rested on her hips and squeezed. Hard. Then he began pumping her up and down with his arms. Sitting up she continued her show while she rode him careful not to make him move too much and cause him pain. She hated that he was in pain.

She watched his face closely and when his eyes bore into hers, she smiled, rocked her hips a few times then continued her up and down movements. Her skin heated, her body tired now, she needed to keep going to finish what she'd started.

Not sure where to put her hands since his chest was laced with bruises, he held his hands up for her to grasp and she locked her fingers in his. His arms offered her the support she needed to hasten her movements. The feel of him sliding in and out of her was the best feeling in the world. He'd always filled her perfectly.

A fire roared through her and settled between her legs and when she dropped down onto him again, her orgasm burned through her as fast a brush fire. Hot and quick.

She gasped and his hands unlocked from hers and clamped onto her hips as his hips rose up to meet her. The groan from deep in his chest escaped and his eyes closed as the expression of ecstasy formed on his lips. Simply. Amazing.

She dropped down over him, her elbows resting next to his ears, her face nestled in the soft space between his shoulder and his neck. The musk of his scent filled her lungs and his arms wrapped around her. There was no place on earth she'd rather be than right here, right now.

The sound of a motorcycle revving up outside caught

her attention and she sat up and looked over her shoulder to the front of the house. Another motorcycle joined the first and then a third.

She rolled off Chase and he rolled over to find an easier position to help him sit up. Opting for lying on his stomach and letting his legs touch the floor, he then used his arms to lift himself up. She watched his fine ass as he walked to his dresser and pulled clean underwear from the top drawer, a new t-shirt and a pair of jeans and walk to the bathroom. She took that time to clean herself up and get dressed. And the music of the motorcycles out front continued to grow.

Her hair fell over her shoulders as she stepped from the bedroom and walked toward the living room. Chase soon joined her at the window where they saw a large group of bikes, many of them from Rolling Thunder, stopped in the street out front.

Smiling Chase opened the front door and stepped outside and waived to his friends, who waived back, some of them walking up the lawn to meet him halfway. She stayed put. They came here to see him before the Veteran's Ride, and it was bad enough he had to miss it this year, she wasn't going to spoil his little time with friends. Backing away from the window she walked to the kitchen and began making breakfast. Their coffee now cold was gathered, poured out and new coffee replaced it.

Pulling her egg bake from the oven, she set it on top to set. The sound of the motorcycles revving outside caught her attention and she stepped into the living room but stayed away from the window to watch Chase wave goodbye to his friends. He watched as they pulled away from him, down the street and then out of sight. Today would be hard for him; he'd never missed a single ride with

Rolling Thunder. At least this wasn't her fault. But she still felt some guilt over it.

He entered the house, walking a bit slower than before, his head down and she wanted to cry for him.

Trying to lighten the mood, she said, "That was really nice of them."

"It was. I have great friends."

36

Chase huffed out a tired but proud breath as he set the weights down on the bar.

"You've done great this week with your therapy. You're almost at 100%. How are your headaches?"

Wiping the sweat from his face with the white towel the therapist handed him, he chuckled. "Better, I only had one day this past week that I had a dull headache."

"That's wonderful."

He watched as the therapist, a man about 10 years younger than himself, wrote in his chart. After writing a few sentences, he looked up at Chase. "That's it for us today. Did you want to schedule your next appointment before you go?"

"I'll have to give you a call to schedule it. I'm heading for Colorado tomorrow for a few days."

"Sounds awesome. Have a great time and give us a call when you know your schedule moving forward."

"Will do."

Walking out of the building to his truck he smiled as the bright sun hit his skin and warmed him. He'd been in a bit of a funk this past week. Missing his first Rolling Thunder Veteran's ride had gotten him down.

Climbing into his rented truck, he nodded as the sharp pains that had run through him earlier in the week were now replaced with a dull ache and nothing more. He'd pulled muscles in his upper back during the accident and the therapy was helping tremendously with that. The trembling in his hands that he'd had in the hospital were completely gone and he was now getting excited for the trip to Durango. Though he'd vacillated over this past week about whether he was doing the right thing, he and LuAnn had decided to go and check out the area and Chief's and talk about it after.

As he left the clinic parking lot, he made a snap decision to stop at Rolling Thunder and see what was happening there. He and Dog needed to have a conversation, their last one was not something that sat well with him and Dog deserved better from him.

Pulling into the Rolling Thunder lot he saw Dog's truck parked close to the backdoor and Joci's Jeep alongside and thought it might be a great time to sit and chat with both of them.

Walking into the garage he was happy to see Ryder working away on a bike. Ryder turned his head and smiled when he saw Chase. Quickly separating the distance, when they were close both of them stuck out their hands and shook, then hugged quickly.

"Nice to see you up and walking."

"Thanks. It feels fantastic to walk and not be in pain. How was the Veteran's Ride?"

"It was good. No issues, raised a lot of money to add an addition on to Donaldson's house and do some small repairs for a few other veterans."

"That's fantastic." He looked toward the door that led to

the store and the staircase that led up to Dog and Joci's office. "Your dad here?"

"Yeah. They're upstairs."

Nodding he turned and walked to the door. Taking a sharp right just outside the door he ascended the stairs that led him to the top floor. His stomach knotted a bit and his heart hammered.

Knocking on the closed office door, Dog's voice sounded, "Come in."

Stepping into the office he saw Dog sitting at his desk working on his computer. Dog looked up at him and stood extending his hand.

"Chase, good to see you up and about."

"It feels good to be up. Do you have a minute?"

"Of course. Sit down. Joci's changing Maddie's diaper in the other room." He pointed to Joci's office, which had been added up here when they married.

Chase sat on the black leather sofa across from Dog's desk and sighed.

"Dog, I wanted to talk about our last conversation. I feel bad about how that ended."

"I do as well, Chase. I overreacted when I saw LuAnn, and while you know what our feelings are about her, it wasn't my place to forbid her from being there. And, you can thank Joci for that bit of clarity. Of all of us here, Joci is the one that has been the most mature about all of this."

Stunned at how this had turned out, Chase smiled. "Thank you for that. Both of you..." The door opened and Joci walked in with Madison, who was now just two years old.

Setting Maddie on the floor so she could walk around the office, Joci closed the door so she was partially contained and smiled when she saw Chase.

"Chase, it's so good to see you. How are you feeling?"

"Much better. Thank you."

The office door burst open and Molly, Emma, Ryder and Gunnar all walked in. Molly had been crying and Emma's eyes were swollen as if she had been.

"What's going on here?" Dog asked.

Gunnar looked at the women first then back to his dad. "The florist shop that Molly and Emma bought our wedding flowers from was destroyed last night in a fire. There's nothing left."

Emma then spoke up. "We've been calling places all morning to find another florist to help us, but the other events in the area this weekend have taken up all of their resources."

Molly's tears started again. "We've put our weddings off for two years now for one thing or another. It's beginning to feel like we're cursed."

Joci came around the desk and hugged Molly, then Emma. "We'll figure something out. I'm sure there's an answer."

Chase, thinking this could be a way for LuAnn to pay them back for some of the grief she'd caused them, said, "LuAnn can do it. She has a supplier out of the area, and she can get some of the most unusual flowers." He looked at the women. "You've seen her work. You know she's good."

Emma's tears trickled down her face. "Gunnar said we couldn't call her."

Joci responded first. "Gunnar, honey, I know this is hard, but please let's not hold this grudge."

"How can you just forgive her? How can you think letting her in, even a little, is okay?"

Joci walked to her son and hugged him. After a few moments she stepped back. "Holding the grudge is harder on you than LuAnn. I'll never be her friend. I'll never trust her again. I'll never want her to be around here with us on a regular basis, but this might be a way, a small way, to help heal some of this pain we all feel when we hear her name."

"How on earth can you be so forgiving?" Gunnar's astonishment was clear.

"Because it's exhausting being mad all the time. Look what we all have here." She looked around the room at all of them. "Let's see if she can help us."

Molly said, "She's done her time, she tried to apologize, can't you give her a chance? She'll never be welcome with open arms, but we can be cordial, if for no other reason, to make things a little easier for Chase." She looked over at him and smiled.

Chase pulled his phone from his back pocket and pulled up LuAnn's number. Standing, he nodded and stepped from the office as the rest of them stayed inside.

"Hi, how was therapy?"

"Good. Hey, I have a favor to ask. A huge favor."

37

LuAnn listened as her heart hammered in her chest.

"They want me to do the flowers for their wedding?"

"Emma and Molly loved the flowers you did at the farmers market. And they're in a bind. I won't lie, Gunnar and Ryder are less than thrilled, but to make the girls happy, they'll allow it. This is your chance, Lu, to make up for some of the trouble you caused."

Tears streamed down her face. She knew she'd caused them trouble, much more than trouble. Everyone knew it. But to hear it come from Chase's mouth, like this, in their defense. Well, it hurt.

She took a breath and cleared her throat. "I won't be able to go to Colorado with you."

"I'll postpone until after the wedding."

She took another large breath and let it out slowly. "Can they come to Forget Me Nots today to go over what they want?"

"I'll check. Thanks, Lu, I'm happy you'll have this chance to ease some tensions."

"Okay. See if they can come in today to allow us time to get the flowers here from my wholesaler."

"Okay."

He hung up and her hands shook. It felt like everything was riding on this. Her whole future. How they'd perceive her in years to come. How she'd perceived herself. But mostly, it felt like her relationship with Chase was riding on this more than anything.

***

Putting the last of their new shipment into the cooler, LuAnn sighed. It had been a hellacious day. The fire in town had swamped them with new orders. Luckily they had a shipment that had been delivered an hour ago and that would get them through a couple of days. Jan had called their supplier and doubled an order to get them through the funerals and weddings scheduled for the weekend and into next week.

"LuAnn?" She jumped and turned to see Jan standing in the cooler doorway.

"I'm sorry, I didn't hear you."

"It's alright. Your brides are here."

"Thank you, Jan. I'll just wash my hands and be right up."

Walking to the sink in the back of the storeroom, she washed as much of the dirt and green stains from her hands as possible. Drying them on a paper towel, she walked to the front of the store to see Molly and Emma standing at the counter looking as nervous as she felt.

"Hi. I guess I should formerly introduce myself. I'm LuAnn Mason."

She held her hand out and first the blond woman extended her hand. "I'm Emma Drake. Fiancé to Gunnar."

"Nice to meet you, Emma."

The dark-haired woman then reached out her hand to shake and said, "I'm Molly Bates, marrying Ryder."

"Nice to meet you. I'll say this, you Sheppards are an amazing looking family. Your wedding pictures are going to be outstanding."

The women giggled nervously but LuAnn continued quickly.

"Why don't we sit down and discuss what you're looking for and see what I'm able to procure for you so we can come up with a plan."

She led them to the office area where they met with clients who needed a bit of privacy.

"Let's start by telling me what you had ordered previously, and I'll see how closely we can recreate it."

She listened to Molly and Emma chatting about the flowers and their dreams of their wedding. The plethora of planning that had gone into it and changing it a couple of times for the birth of a baby and a trial, she felt for these gals. Though thoughts of a wedding had never been something LuAnn had dreamed of, except in her demented state when she'd thought one day she'd be married to Jeremiah, she'd not thought past the present in years.

"Okay. So, I can get some of these." She flipped a page in the catalogue and pointed to another variety of rose. "I can get these in silver and red. I'll fill in with the spider mums, greens and ivy. Anything else?"

Emma broke down in tears one more time and Molly rubbed her back. "Hey Em, it's all good. This is it. We loved her flowers at the farmers market and were a tiny bit sad that we'd already ordered our flowers. Now, we're getting something totally unique and it's going to be fabulous."

Emma swiped under her eyes. "I know. These are tears of joy. And relief."

LuAnn smiled at both of them. "I'm sorry you've been so stressed, but I've got this. I'll call you when the flowers get here tomorrow and if you want to come and see them, you're welcome to do that. By Saturday, they'll be ready. I can get them to you wherever you'd like them."

Her stomach twisted when Molly and Emma looked at each other. Emma opened her mouth then closed it.

Trying again she softly said, "I don't know what to say. You know tensions being what they are..."

LuAnn held up her hand, her bottom lip quivered, and her voice shook.

"Please don't worry. I won't go there and make anyone nervous. This is my small way of trying to apologize for nearly getting Joci and the baby killed. It wasn't my intention, but that doesn't matter. I didn't know Joci was pregnant, but that doesn't matter, either. I did it. I'm sorry and ashamed for what I've done."

Her eyes welled with tears. She cleared her throat and tried to smile but it was stiff and forced.

"We have a delivery driver that will drop them at the church for you. Or your home, wherever you want them delivered."

"Holy Family Church would be perfect," Molly said.

LuAnn shakily wrote Holy Family on the order form and swallowed.

"Okay. Anything else?"

Molly pulled her purse up on the table. "We just need to pay."

"Jan, our owner, said the flowers are on her. She's helping out everyone. The design work of putting the bouquets and boutonnières together is on me as a way of saying I'm sorry."

"Oh, no you don't have..." Emma started but LuAnn stood.

"Honestly. It's the least we can do."

Emma and Molly stood, and LuAnn stepped from the office and waited for them to exit the door. To her surprise, Emma pulled her in for a hug and whispered, "Thank you."

Molly did the same and she stood silent and stunned as she watched the two beautiful women walk out the door.

38

Chase's pride for LuAnn grew as he watched her set each arrangement neatly into a box on Saturday morning. He'd come to the shop to help her gather everything together and he'd agreed to deliver the flowers himself. He was amazed by the care with which she placed each bouquet, corsage and boutonniere into the box, surrounded by tissue paper so they didn't get smashed.

"Okay. I think I've got everything in these four boxes." She stood and rubbed her hands together. "I'm nervous."

He walked to her and pulled her close. "Lu, they look fantastic. They will be a hit for sure."

He kissed her lips, hugged her tight and waited until she pulled away first.

"Okay, let's get them loaded into the truck."

He took one box, and she took another as they walked to his truck. Actually, his loaner while his case was being settled; there was no question of liability so he should receive a nice recovery for his truck and his damages. His insurance company might be paying for the loaner, but it would be reimbursed by the drunk driver's company shortly. It was a spectacular truck. Likely the reason the dealerships offered beautiful new loaners. It was hard to buy lesser of a vehicle once you drove something like this.

Setting the boxes side by side in the backseat, they turned to grab the last two boxes. Laying them carefully on the floor of the backseat, LuAnn turned to him.

"Thank you for delivering these. We appreciate it."

"It's selfish on my part. I want to be there when they see them and show them what you can do."

She giggled. "Thank you." Her cheeks turned pink and he loved the light that brought to her face.

"Okay, I'm off. I'll see you at home in about an hour. Then, how about we dress up, we'll drop a gift off at the wedding, then we'll go out to a nice dinner."

"As long as you mean that you'll run the gift in and I'll stay in the car, that's a solid yes."

"That's exactly what I meant. I'm not interested in the drama, either."

He kissed her lips, then her nose, then climbed into his truck.

The drive to the Church was filled with thoughts of what was, what could be and what he wanted out of life. Greg had told him to have some quiet moments for reflection. Normally, those came on the back of his bike, but he wasn't cleared by the doctors for riding yet. Though, he hoped it would be pretty damned soon. He missed it.

So, what was? They all knew of LuAnn's past obsession with Dog and how she had misconstrued his care of her to be more than friendship. She'd admitted feeling stupid about that now. She'd not allowed for anything else in her mind. Even though he'd been right there the whole time. It was maddening. But, you can't control your heart. He tried. He tried dating others while she was in prison. His heart just wouldn't let go. That brought him to what could be.

It could be that he and LuAnn were able to find a way to get the Rolling Thunder crew to accept that she's around. It could be that over time, more time, hearts would soften. Hate would fade. And a simple acceptance of he and LuAnn together would be had. But, that would take years. Many more years. And then there was what did he want?

He wanted the opportunity to design and build bikes. His very own custom bikes. Hadn't Dog instilled that in him? JT too? They were all together in the garage as Dog built his first bike, then his next one. He was right there when Dog opened Rolling Thunder. He'd put together more bikes from frame up than anyone he knew outside of JT. Then he and JT started messing around with designing them. Adding this piece and that and customers loved them. Then JT designed a bike on his own and took it to Sturgis and did well with it. He didn't come in first, but close enough that he got attention and the business grew from there. He wanted that. He wanted to ride down the highway and see a Chase Matthews design riding the road with him. It made his heart sing to think of that happening. To stop at an event where there were thousands of bikes and to see one of his designs, or more, parked along with the other great bikes out there. But that also would take years. Dog knew what made his business successful and he was hard pressed to change it much, and if he did, no matter Chase's contributions to the designs, the credit would always go to the Head Designer, JT. Chase would never be Head Designer at Rolling Thunder. Couldn't blame Dog, but where did that leave him? He also liked thinking about a future with LuAnn. Maybe a kid or two. A dog would be nice. A family. He hadn't had his own family for a long time. His mom took off when he was young, and his dad was a drunk. There was a time when he thought he shouldn't have his own kids because he had bad genes. But, shit, he'd turned out pretty damned good. He'd pass that on and be there for his kids. Show them the right way to do things. Love them. That's all he really wanted in this whole life. He wanted to be loved.

LuAnn loved him. He loved her. He loved Dog and JT and Ryder, too, but he loved her more. It was simply that easy to say.

Pulling into the parking lot of the church, he saw Ryder walking across the parking lot with his tuxedo on a hangar slung over his shoulder. He looked happy. He was marrying the woman of his dreams. She'd helped him through some of his shyness and they were good together. He was happy for Ryder and Gunnar. But he wanted that for himself too. And, he wanted them to be happy for him.

Parking he stepped from the truck, opened the back-door and pulled out the first box of flowers. Closing the door, he carried them into the church and down the steps to the classrooms where the girls were likely getting ready. Seeing Joci in the hall with Maddie he called to her.

"Hi Joci, where should I put the flowers?"

"Oh, hi Chase. How about we set them over here on the table by the counter."

She walked to the table and moved programs sitting in a stack. They had two hours before the ceremony. Maddie toddled over to them laughing and he couldn't help but smile at her. She was adorable.

"I have three more boxes." But, since he wanted to see Joci's face, he opened the box so she could see the gorgeous array of flowers.

"Oh, my heavens. Those are simply stunning." She exclaimed.

Her fingers gently brushed over some of the vibrant red and silver petals.

Molly came into the room and walked right up to them. "Oh my God. Those are simply fabulous. Oh, Chase, tell LuAnn these are just absolutely perfect."

She picked up one of the corsages and turned it slowly, to and fro, to see each of the delicate flowers tucked into the arrangement.

"I will. I'll go get the rest of them."

Each time he carried a box down the steps more of the women had arrived to look at the flowers. Dog's mom and sisters-in-law were all happily exclaiming about the beauty of the flowers and how much they admired them. His heart swelled and he couldn't wait to tell LuAnn.

Finally, the last box was laid on the table and Emma quickly opened it to see the two bridal bouquets.

"Ohh." She stood still, her hands over her mouth staring at the bouquets.

Finally, with shaking fingers, she picked up one of the bouquets and brought it up to her nose. Inhaling, her eyes closed. and she sighed.

Molly stepped forward and picked up the other bouquet and both women smiled brighter than the sun.

Molly looked at Chase, a tear rolling down her cheek, "Please tell LuAnn, these are perfect. And, thank you."

"I will. See you all later."

Chase walked out of the church, feeling such pride and admiration for the fact that LuAnn, worked so hard for people who had not treated her well, though with good reasons. It felt like the perfect piece to this puzzle. He was excited to tell LuAnn.

Her stomach was in knots with worry and excitement. The job she'd done on those flowers was outstanding. Pulling up her phone, she sent photos of the arrangements to her supplier.

Then she cleaned up the backroom, got in her car and headed for Chase's house. They'd have to have the conversation about when she'd go back to Linda's now that he was feeling better.

Setting about finishing up their laundry until Chase returned, she was humming as she folded his shirts. She rather liked this domestic chore. Touching his clothing and keeping things neat for him made her feel like she was helping him.

The door opened and Chase walked in from the garage, stopped in the doorway and leaned against the frame. She turned and smiled at him, one of his black t-shirts in her hands.

"Just finishing up. How did it go?"

He smiled at her then, his gorgeous dark brown eyes even twinkled a bit, his handsome face was a sight to behold. He filled the doorway completely and looked relaxed.

"I love watching you here. You should stay."

"I was just thinking we needed to have that conversation."

"You should stay. I love having you here."

"Is it too soon?"

He stepped forward, his right hand cupped the nape of her head and pulled her forward. "You should stay. I want you to stay."

His lips covered hers, softly yet completely, his tongue delved into her mouth and swirled around. Her tongue danced with his. Her arms wrapped around his waist and held him close.

Pulling back slightly, she replied. "I want to stay."

Kissing his lips once more she stepped back. "Wow."

"Yeah."

She finished folding his shirt, so she didn't wrinkle it. "Tell me, please."

Setting his shirt on the pile she turned to face him.

"They were speechless. They loved them. Even Joci said to say thank you the flowers were perfect."

She let out a long breath. Tears sprang to her eyes and she sniffed. "Thank God."

She leaned against the dryer, her body needed support, her legs threatened to buckle under her the relief was so powerful.

Chase chuckled and his eyes held humor and love. It was impossible not to see it. She even recognized it now. She hoped he could see in her eyes how much she loved him.

"So, what needs to happen here today? Should we go and shop for a wedding gift, then we can come home and dress up to go out. I feel like we should celebrate."

She giggled. "That sounds fantastic. I just want to finish folding this load, so they don't wrinkle."

Chase kissed her nose and stepped from the laundry room to the kitchen. She could hear him putting the breakfast dishes in the dishwasher. They'd left in such a hurry this morning the kitchen was still a bit of a mess. She continued to fold his clothes, her thoughts happy that she'd done a good job for the Sheppards and at the possibilities the future held. She'd be moving in with Chase and that felt fantastic. Her future, for the first time in a long time, felt secure. She had direction. A good job doing something she loved to do and above all else, she had Chase.

Taking the folded laundry from the top of the dryer, she carried it to the bedroom and began filling his dresser with the fresh clean clothes. Chase entered the room behind her and looked around.

"How many drawers do you need?"

She glanced over at him and saw him looking around the room as if to figure this out. "I don't have much for clothes. Just a couple of drawers should work."

"I have plenty of room in the closet, so we should be good there. What else am I not thinking of?"

Laughing she answered. "You've thought more about this than I have. I guess a shelf and a drawer in the bathroom would be nice."

"Oh, the bathroom. I'm on it."

He left the room and she laughed again. This was exciting.

She heard Chase's phone ring and he answered it.

"Yeah, what about next week?"

Remembering Colorado, she stopped what she was doing and listened. Walking to the bathroom where he stood looking out the window, the array of items he'd pulled from his cabinet sitting on the counter, she leaned against the door frame and waited for him to finish his call.

Pocketing his phone, he turned to see her standing in the door. "Want to go to Colorado next week?"

"Sure." She smiled at him. She loved the excitement in his eyes, the new exuberance in his actions. "I thought maybe you'd changed your mind about going."

He walked to her, lay his hands on her shoulders and looked into her eyes. "Greg asked me to figure out what I really wanted from my life. What could be. I love Dog. I love the guys too and I love my job. But, I have more to offer than what Dog has available for me. Honestly speaking, if I don't explore this offer, I'm holding myself back. I don't want to do that. It would be different if Dog had a design job available at the money I'm being offered or close to it even if I would never be Head Designer and I was snubbing my nose at it."

"That's true. And you're amazing at what you do."

"Plus," He leaned against the bathroom counter, resting his fine butt on the edge, "I want you in my life. Even though you did the flowers today, it will never be comfortable for you around them or vice versa."

"Emma and Molly seemed very nice when we met."

"They are and they weren't around when everything went down with you, so they don't have the hard feelings, but let's face it, they will never be your friends, it would be too complicated."

"Right." Her stomach tightened. It was hard to hear it. Taking a deep breath, she tried getting her head around everything. Did it even pay for her to move in here only to have to move again if they did?

"So, when do we leave?"

"Gil is arranging the tickets, probably tomorrow to fly in and enjoy our evening. Monday morning I'd tour the facility. I'd like you to come with me. You worked for years at Rolling Thunder, so you'd understand it all. Gil even said he'd find a job for you there if you wanted one."

She laughed out loud. "Well, we'll see. I'd actually prefer to find another florist or greenhouse to work at though." She turned to finish putting Chase's clothes away. "We better get going, we have to find wedding gifts and go out, later we'll be packing."

40

Chase pulled into a parking spot and put the truck in park. LuAnn smiled at him and handed him the beautifully wrapped presents they'd purchased for Ryder and Molly and Gunnar and Emma.

He leaned over and kissed her. "I won't be long." She was beautiful tonight. Actually, every night, but tonight she'd dressed up, curled her hair rather than pulling it back into a ponytail; she wore makeup, though just light touches, enough to accent the blue in her eyes.

"Thank you." She softly replied.

After stepping down from the truck, he closed the door, winked at LuAnn and walked to the reception venue. He wanted to shake Ryder and Gunnar's hands, hug Molly and Emma and say hi to Dog before taking LuAnn out to dinner. It was the best compromise he could think of and it would have to do.

Entering the venue, which opened to the bar on the left and the dining area later to become the dance floor on the right. Tables were set and people were milling about chatting, laughing and celebrating. As it should be.

He only had a slight pang in his heart at not being able to totally celebrate with his friends who were also his family.

"Chase, so glad to see you." Emma walked up to him and hugged him tight.

He reciprocated with a one-armed hug holding the packages with the other.

"You look stunning, Emma."

She laughed. "It's finally here, can you believe it? I'm Mrs. Gunnar Shepard."

"When it's meant to be, it happens. You've all earned it with everything you've managed to get through to be here."

Gunnar walked toward them. He looked handsome in his tuxedo. His dark hair had grown out again after buzzing it off three years ago and he looked both rugged and refined.

Gunnar reached his hand out first to shake Chase's and the warm welcome feelings that flooded his heart almost overwhelmed him. Firmly shaking Gunnar's hand, he leaned in and half hugged his friend. He needed to put these packages somewhere.

Joci walked up to them and softly said, "Let me set these down for you."

She took the packages and carried them to the gift table.

Reaching his left arm around Gunnar, Chase hugged him close.

"Congratulations, man."

"Thank you. It's long overdue, but it makes it feel sweeter for some reason."

"I'll bet."

Gunnar wrapped his arm around Emma's shoulders and pulled her close.

"Hey, there you are." Molly and Ryder walked up hand

in hand. He leaned down and hugged Molly first, then repeated the hug he'd given Gunnar.

"You're a gorgeous bride, Molly."

"Hey, what about me?" Ryder teased.

"You're not a bride and are as ugly as ever." Chase teased back.

"Fuck you." Ryder jibbed.

Gunnar interrupted. "What are you drinking, Chase, I'll get you one."

Holding up his hand to stave off any comments, he said, "I can't stay. I'm on my way to dinner and we wanted to drop this off beforehand."

Gunnar's smile dropped but Emma chimed in quickly. "That's lovely, thank you. And, please thank LuAnn again for the spectacular job she did on the flowers."

He nodded, "I'll do that."

Looking at Ryder and Gunnar he nodded, "I'd like to say hi to Dog and Joci before I leave."

Ryder patted him on the shoulder. "They're over by the gift table with Grandma and Grandpa."

"Congratulations again to all of you."

Stepping away, his heart felt heavy, but he knew it was the right thing to do. He walked up to Joci and Dog and Joci's smile was genuine and welcoming.

"Chase, you look great. Are you feeling better?"

"I am, thank you." He gave Joci a quick hug and turned to look Dog in the eyes. There was a sadness there and it made him feel even worse.

Dog reached out his hand and their eyes locked. Taking Dog's hand in his, he shook as firmly as he could causing Dog's lips to lift in the corners. It was how Dog had taught him to shake hands.

"Congratulations on your two new daughters."

"Thank you for coming, Chase. It wouldn't be the same

without you."

Chase rubbed the nape of his neck, "I'm not staying, Dog. We're going out to eat. This was the best compromise I could think of for all parties involved."

Dog swallowed a large lump in his throat, then nodded slightly.

He turned to see Joci watching Dog very closely. "Congratulations, Joci, and sorry I didn't say it before, but you look beautiful."

She lifted on her toes and wrapped her arms around him. "You look dashing yourself."

Turning back to Dog, he said, "I'll be out of town next week. So, I'll be using my vacation days. I'll be healed up and feel my old self after that."

"Of course, Chase. Your health is more important than anything. Travel safe."

Guilt filled his stomach, but he couldn't say anything just now. He didn't even know if he'd like it out there. Maybe he'd hate the shop or maybe Gil wasn't being truthful or maybe the area wouldn't work for them. The what ifs continued to circle his head.

"I'll see you all in a week. Enjoy your celebration, you have much to celebrate."

"That we do." Dog nodded, reached his hand out once again and Chase gladly shook it.

Nodding to Joci, he turned and headed to the door.

Stepping outside, he inhaled deeply and let it out slowly. That all felt clumsy, awkward and hard. It left a bitter taste in his mouth and he didn't like it.

As he walked to the back of the parking lot toward the truck he heard a woman scream. "Help."

He hastened his steps, still unable to run from his accident, toward the woman screaming. "Help. Someone. Help."

41

LuAnn sat in the truck and looked over the parking lot at the plethora of vehicles parked there. They had a fantastic turnout for their weddings. Good for them. Her stomach tightened at the thought that she was keeping Chase from his friends and surrogate family. She sure hated to do that. When he got back to the truck, she'd offer, once again, to go home and let him have his fun with this part of his life. They would have their time in Colorado to have a nice evening out and celebrate.

Sitting up straighter, so her dress didn't wrinkle she looked down to her lap and the pretty, medium-blue dress Chase had purchased for her this morning. While they were shopping for wedding gifts, she saw it in the window of a cute little shop and commented on it. He said, "Go try it on."

Her cheeks burned from embarrassment. She wasn't hinting for him to buy it. "It's okay, we should finish finding wedding gifts."

"I insist." He took her by the hand and walked into the store ahead of her. A clerk stood at the doorway, "Hi, welcome. Are you looking for something in particular?" Chase smiled at the clerk, which clearly made her panties wet the way she squirmed. "Yes, I'd like to see that dress," he pointed to the window, "on this gorgeous lady."

The clerk looked at her for the first time and nodded. "What size do you wear, a 2?"

LuAnn's cheeks, still hot, heated further. "I'm actually a 4, because of my bust."

At the same time, both the clerk and Chase looked at her breasts and she wanted to crawl in a hole.

Walking to a rack to her left, the clerk pulled the dress from the bar and headed to the back of the store. "Follow me, I'll get you a dressing room."

A quick glance at Chase's handsome face and his beautiful smile, she followed the clerk feeling rather self-conscious.

"Here you go. Just let me know if you need a different size."

Closing the door behind her, she pulled her t-shirt over her head, kicked off her sandals and shimmied her jeans over her hips. Pulling the dress from the hangar, she easily slid it over her head and watched in the mirror as the soft shimmery fabric slid down her body in a cloud of blue. The length stopped just above her knees. The stretchy material hugged her breasts and flowed over her hips. She turned back and forth and loved how the fabric floated in the air. She'd never had anything so nice before.

Glancing at the tag hanging under her arm she saw the price and winced. It wasn't exorbitant, but she'd never pay that much for a dress.

"Come out here, Lu and let me look at you." Chase's voice called behind the door.

Stepping from the doorway, she saw him waiting for her. His gorgeous form leaned slightly as he perched his elbow on a clothing rack across from the dressing room. His eyes were fixed on her body. His tanned skin and dark brown eyes were the most mesmerizing sight she'd ever seen. Her thoughts instantly went back to this morning and their lovemaking and how he felt sliding inside of her body. Now she was the one who was wet.

"It's perfect." He turned to the salesclerk standing alongside him. "We'll take it."

"But, Chase, it's a bit..."

"Stop. You look fantastic in this dress. It's the color of the bike I'm going to build - Metamorphosis."

When she'd put it on this evening fresh from the shower, he'd bent down to his knees before her, shimmied her dress up and her panties down and immediately placed his lips on her pussy. Sucking her in and massaging her with his tongue, she came fast, her knees threatening to buckle under her.

He stood then, kissed her lips and whispered, "Tonight, it's my turn. I'll be thinking about it all night."

Sexiest. Man. Ever.

Smoothing the fabric, she looked across the parking lot once more and saw two little girls walking toward the swampy area on the other side of the lot. A quick look around for parents or sitters proved fruitless.

Unbuckling her seatbelt, she opened the truck door, still watching for adults with these girls. Quickly walking across the parking lot, she kept her eyes on the girls while also trying to see an adult somewhere.

Walking as quickly as she could in her heels, she didn't want to yell and scare the girls; but she felt almost certain that the girls didn't know there was a pond hidden in the long grass where they were headed. As the girls neared the edge of the parking lot, LuAnn picked up her pace, trying to run in her heels. Fearful she wouldn't make it in time, she took her shoes off, and carried them in her hand, trying to dodge stones in the parking lot as she ran toward the girls.

The girls disappeared into a thicket of cattails and her heart raced. Where were their parents?

Another quick glance and no adults. Hearing a splash and a scream, LuAnn took off at a full run to get there and save the little girls.

High pitched squealing came between splashes of water. LuAnn dropped her shoes before entering the tall grass and yelled to the girls. "I'm coming. Where are you?"

Splashing was all she heard. Seeing the water before her, and where the splashing was coming from, LuAnn jumped into the mucky water and swam to the closest girl who was thrashing about. Grabbing her by the waist she tried calming her while wildly looking around for the other little girl. "It's okay, I've got you."

The water deepened and she was now trying to swim with one arm. Finally seeing the other little girl bobbing near the tall grasses she turned in that direction and yelled as loud as she could. "Help." Getting closer but seeing the little girl go under she yelled again. "Help. Someone. Help."

Hearing footsteps running toward her, she continued to swim through the muck to the little girl whose crying had turned to coughing and gagging.

"What the fuck?"

Looking up she saw Chase. "They fell in. Can you reach the little one?"

She tried pointing while also trying to stay above the water. The little one in her arm cried. "I want my momma."

"I'll get you there, sweetie." LuAnn huffed. She was growing tired but close to the edge now.

Chase reached down and pulled the littler girl from the water. Turning her over he patted her back to get the water from her lungs.

LuAnn reached the edge, hoisted the girl she had in her arms to the edge of the water and grabbed onto the long grasses to pull herself from the water. Voices from the parking lot could be heard, "Maddie. Dakota."

Chase yelled, "Over here."

LuAnn checked over the little girl she'd pulled from the water. She was coughing and crying at the same time and LuAnn patted her back and told her it would be alright.

"What the hell did you do?"

She looked up to see Jeremiah scowling down at her. "I didn't do anything."

"Were you trying to drown them?"

"Of course not. Why would I do that?" She felt panicked that they'd think it, and she'd be arrested again. "I saved them." Reaching down for the little girl Chase was with, Jeremiah picked her up and ran up to the edge of the parking lot. Gunnar and JT came to the edge of the parking lot and JT immediately grabbed the little girl she'd helped. "Dakota are you alright?"

Dakota started crying and JT hugged her close.

Soon others came rushing toward them. Ryder said, "I called an ambulance."

Chase walked over to her and reached down to help her up. Her gorgeous dress was ruined and so was her mood. They'd always think the worst of her. Always.

"Tell me what happened, Lu." Chase asked softly.

Her lips quivered. "I was sitting in the truck and I saw them walking across the parking lot. I didn't see any adults following them or anywhere around." Her voice cracked, but she kept going, "I knew about the marsh here and I worried they'd fall in, so I started following them. Before I could get here, they'd fallen in."

Chase's arms wrapped around her shoulders and pulled her close. She softly cried in his arms. Part fear. Part adrenaline. Part sadness at the look Jeremiah had just given her. Joseph was right, a new start was in order.

$\mathcal{H}$e held her while she cried. Her body shook, her skin now cold from the water, and she was covered in a green slime that covered the top of the water.

"Hey, it's alright."

She shook her head, and he knew what she meant. Jeremiah had no right. None. He'd accused her of trying to drown the little girls. Chase's jaw hurt from clenching it so tightly.

The sirens could be heard in the distance and he pulled away slightly. A crowd at the edge of the pond gathered. Gooseflesh formed on LuAnn's skin. He looked down at her and saw her makeup had smeared under her eyes; her hair which had been curled now hung in wet strands with a soft covering of green on them and her dress. That sexy flowing dress now wet and dirty clung to her body. Her nipples were visible against the soft fabric and while he liked that, he didn't want anyone else looking at her.

Unbuttoning his black dress shirt, he pulled it off,

leaving the black t-shirt on and draped it around LuAnn's shoulders.

She looked up at him, her bright smile gone. "I'm so sorry I ruined my new dress."

"Don't you be sorry, Lu. You just saved two little girls from drowning. You're a hero. We can replace the dress. Those little one's can't be replaced. You did the right thing."

Her sad smile said it all.

He turned, his arm around her waist and began walking them up to the parking lot. Two ambulances pulled into the lot and stopped at the edge of the marsh. Rescue workers jumped from the truck and asked people to step aside so they could help the victims. Once they reached the top of the marsh, alongside the parking lot, they both paused to watch and make sure the little girls were going to be okay.

A squad car pulled in behind the ambulances and an officer approached them.

"I'm going to need to ask you a few questions."

LuAnn nodded. "Okay."

She slowly recounted what had happened. Her shivering continued and the officer stopped taking her statement and opened his trunk. Coming back to them with a solar blanket, he opened it up and handed it to him. Chase happily wrapped it around LuAnn and pulled her close. As much for support as warmth.

The officer closed his notepad. "I'll need you to stay here for a moment while I talk to the family."

LuAnn nodded but turned her sad eyes to his. "Chase, I didn't try to hurt them. I don't want to go to jail. I didn't do anything wrong." Her lip quivered and tears sprung to her eyes.

"Hey, I know you didn't do anything to hurt them and you aren't going to go to jail."

"But...Dog...." She stopped talking as the sobs clogged her throat.

"LuAnn?"

JT's wife, Kayden's voice, had them both turning their heads.

"Dakota told me what happened. Thank you so much for saving my daughter." Tears rolled down her cheeks as she looked over at JT holding Dakota. "We have a sitter, but apparently she met a boy." Kayden wiped her eyes and JT walked over holding Dakota who was also wrapped in a solar blanket. His jaw was clenched but that could be the whole situation, LuAnn, or just the fear of what had happened. He wrapped his free arm around Kayden and pulled her close.

JT looked up at Dakota and nodded. Dakota turned her head, her hair looked much the same as LuAnn's except for the lighter color. Her sweet face was smudged with muck and dirt though you could see someone tried washing it.

"Thank you." Dakota sweetly said to LuAnn.

LuAnn burst out crying and hugged Dakota, which cause JT's jaw to tighten further.

"I'm so happy you're okay," LuAnn said between breaths. Kayden hugged LuAnn from the side and they had a brief but tender moment.

Kayden cleared her throat and stepped back. "I just want to thank you for saving them. I don't know what I would have done if..."

Unable to finish the sentence JT finally took a deep breath. "Thanks, LuAnn. We do appreciate what you've done for us. For our family."

They turned and walked away, and LuAnn stared after them in what appeared to be disbelief. She looked up at him again, her face now clean where the tears had streamed down and wiped the dirt away.

"LuAnn?" Dog's voice was gruff.

LuAnn turned to face him, her body shook, and he wrapped his arms tighter around her to show her support. He was still damn pissed at Dog for accusing her of drowning, so he'd better not say another word at this moment.

"I apologize about accusing you of drowning the girls. I'll work on not always expecting the worst from you. That's on me. And, thank you for saving my little Maddie. It would have killed us to lose her. She means the...world." His voice cracked with emotion but before waiting for a response, he turned and walked to Joci and Maddie, who was still being attended to by an EMT.

The police officer walked back over and nodded. "I don't have any other questions for you, Ms. Mason. You'll likely want to get home and clean up. Thank you for being here to help these girls out. You've done a hero's work today and we thank you."

He walked toward his squad and LuAnn stared after him. Then she jerked from his arms and called to the officer. "I have your blanket."

"No, ma'am, you keep that."

He nodded and got into his squad car and pulled from the lot as they watched.

"Come on, sweetheart, let's get you home and in the tub. Nothing personal but you sort of stink."

She laughed and that was the response he was looking for. "Maybe I'll join you in the tub with some wine."

"I love the sound of that, Chase."

———

43

*L*uAnn lay back against Chase's chest, his strong legs on either side of her, the steam from the warm water wafting up to the ceiling. She sipped the glass of white wine in her hand and closed her eyes.

"How do you feel about Dog apologizing to you?"

She lifted her right shoulder and let it fall. "He had to; he was wrong. And I'd just saved his daughter's life. And, her life was in danger because no one was watching a two-year-old. I was surprised when he said he was working on not always expecting the worst of me and Joci was helping him."

"Yeah." He took a drink from his glass and set it on the edge of the tub. "Gil called while you were showering. We get on a plane at 9:00 a.m. tomorrow. We'll be there for five days. He's putting us up at a great hotel in downtown. A friend of his owns it, says we can feel free to order room service, the works."

"Wow, he's really going all out for you."

"He sure is."

"How do you feel about that?"

His arms circled her shoulders, his fingertips grazed the water and he sent little ripples shooting across the tub.

"It feels great to be wanted. It feels outstanding to have someone love my bike designs so much that they're willing to go this far to court me. But, I'm cautiously optimistic about the whole thing. We'll see when we get there if this is all much ado about nothing or if this is legit."

"That's a good plan."

She lay her head against his shoulder, "Tell me about the first bike you'll build again."

The sound of his voice, the cadence and quality mesmerized her. After he visited in prison, she'd go to sleep many nights remembering how he sounded when he spoke. The deep tenor floated over her body till she fell asleep. When he laughed, oh, it took her breath away. His smile was perfect. His straight teeth were framed perfectly by his full supple lips.

"I think it'll be perfect."

Pulling herself from her thoughts she smiled. "I think it will, too."

His arms tightened around her and he kissed the side of her head, his whiskers such a contrast to the softness of his lips. It made her nipples pebble and gooseflesh rose on her arms.

"I want this for us, Lu. A fresh start. I'll be able to realize my dream of being a bike designer and builder and make a shit ton of money doing it. You'll be able to do whatever it is you want to do, work for a greenhouse, open your own, it won't matter, there won't be people judging you and shunning you at every turn. We'll both be able to breath. Plus, the weather will be warmer, the scenery stunning and we'll be able to be who we are. I so want this for us."

Setting her wine glass on the edge of the tub, she

turned in his arms and stared into his eyes. She lay her left hand against his cheek, her thumb roving over his lips.

"I wasn't sure at first. I didn't want you to do this for me. That would never work. But, hearing you say it like that. Living your dream. Being free of all of this negativity. Oh, that sounds like the stuff dreams are made of. Doing it with you, that is a dream come true."

She leaned closer and touched her lips to his. It was a soft simple kiss. She wanted to convey her earnestness in his dream for them, sort of seal the deal, but his arms pulled her close, their wet chests came together, the water slightly sloshing around them added a buoyancy to their movements. He slid lower in the water; his thick firm cock pressed against her pussy the water adding a new element to the way their bodies felt together. They'd never made love in a bathtub before.

Raising herself up slightly, his cock bobbed up between her legs easily and she directed it with her left hand as she steadied herself with her right. Never looking away from his eyes, she watched him as she slowly slid down onto him. His pupils dilated and his nostrils flared. His hands encircled her hips and she sat up to seat herself fully. His eyes immediately dropped to her chest and he was enthralled with their movement and she bobbed up and down on him, her wet breasts moving and swaying easily.

Grabbing a breast in each hand she rubbed her forefinger over her nipples, and he licked his lips. He tried leaning forward to suck one in his mouth, but the water caused him to slide forward and he quickly resumed laying back against the tub.

Her right hand reached out and pinched his right nipple, then rolled it between her fingers until it puckered tightly into a small brown bud. Quickly doing the same to the other she smiled as she felt him jerk inside of her.

Raising up and dropping down, careful not to slip, he slowly sat up, reached the drain behind her and pulled it up letting the water begin to drain out.

"I can't do what I want when we're slipping around."

His voice was gruff, his muscles tensed as he gained purchase and began thrusting up into her as she came down on him. He went into her deeper and she slightly moaned not expecting the fullness. His lips turned up into a smile when she groaned, and he did it again and again.

Within a few strokes her orgasm burst through her and she cried out his name as he anchored himself to the back of the tub and lifted his hips, causing her to ride him like a pony. Soon he groaned out his orgasm and his hips jerked and jerked as it seemed to last longer than most.

He lay back exhausted. His arms fell to the tub and she leaned forward pressing her body against his as they each gained their breath, and their breathing became normal again.

44

Stepping off the airplane, he took LuAnn's hand as they walked through the airport terminal toward the baggage claim area. The weather was warmer here, the sun that shown through the windows was high in the sky. He was eager and while he'd told LuAnn he was being cautiously optimistic, he wasn't. He was fucking excited. Each day that passed his vision became clearer, his goal set. This was their time to start anew without old baggage holding them back.

They got on an escalator to the claim floor and as they moved toward the carousel to pick up their luggage, they found themselves dodging people. Finding the correct carousel, they stood along with others from their plane. He recognized the older couple coming to see their kids here. They'd sat across the aisle on the plane from them. The older man looked over at him and nodded, and Chase smiled and waved.

The loud buzzing started, and the carousel began to turn. A few more moments and luggage began to drop on the conveyor. LuAnn ran to the carousel and pulled their small bag from the conveyor. He chuckled but came up behind her, "Lu, just tell me which one and I'll grab it."

She tilted her head back and smiled up at him and his heartbeat increased. So beautiful. Taking the bag from her hand, he stood as she watched the luggage roll past them. There must be several million black suitcases with wheels on them in this world. Luckily, theirs was deep red, easier to spot. And there it was, dropping from the conveyor onto the carousel. LuAnn looked back at him, "I suppose I don't have to tell you which one it is." They both had a good chuckle, and he shook his head. "No, ma'am."

He stepped around her and as the suitcase neared he easily picked it off the carousel.

Setting the suitcase on its wheels he turned to LuAnn, nodded and they began walking toward the exit. She'd been very quiet during most of this trip and he worried she wasn't excited about leaving Wisconsin. Tamping down old lingering feelings of jealousy that she wanted to stay close to Dog, he shook his head of the awful thoughts and focused on the present.

"You're quiet."

Stepping outside she looked up at the sun, the light kissed her skin and she positively glowed. "I am. I'm trying to keep my excitement in check because I don't want to think of this place as better than it actually is. You know, build it up and be sorry later. I'm trying to stay levelheaded about this."

Relief flowed through him and he felt his shoulders relax. "I know what you mean."

Seeing the car rental sign, he turned and pointed. "We have to head that way to pick up our car."

It wasn't far, but the warmth already caused him to sweat just a bit. It felt good.

Entering the rental office, he walked to the counter and

pulled his license from his wallet. The clerk was efficient and had their paperwork in order.

"You need to sign next to all the x's."

Signing his name in multiple places his excitement grew. Almost time to explore. The clerk slid his keys across the counter and pointed to the back of the building.

"You're Jeep is out back, follow the sidewalk. It's the white one. Enjoy your stay."

"Thank you." Picking up the small bag and hoisting it over his shoulder, he turned and saw LuAnn standing at the window holding the handle of the red suitcase.

She turned and smiled at him, her excitement growing by the look in her eyes. He kissed her lips and whispered. "Gil got us a Jeep."

"That's awesome."

Their steps became lighter and they climbed into their new ride for the week. Setting the GPS for the hotel he started the Jeep, looked over at LuAnn, whose smile was brighter than the sun.

"Ready to begin our new adventure?"

"I sure am."

As he drove to the hotel, both he and LuAnn were looking around the area, the buildings and the people sauntering about. Parking in the hotel lot, his heart felt full and happy. A parking attendant rushed to the driver's side of the Jeep and he hopped out, handed the keys over and watched as another attendant began unloading their bags from the back.

This was the first time in his life he'd been treated like this. LuAnn watched from the other side of the vehicle clearly stunned and amused by the look on his face.

His phone rang and he saw Gil's name on the read out.

"Hello."

"Are you here yet?"

He laughed and walked toward LuAnn. Pulling a five-dollar bill from his front pocket, he handed it to the valet and followed the bellhop carrying their bags into the lobby. LuAnn walked alongside of him, her eyes taking everything in.

"We are just walking into the hotel now."

"Great. Just give them my name, I've made all the arrangements. If you want to come out to the shop this evening, we're having a pig roast. It's our anniversary this month, so we're having some doings each weekend. If you're tired and want to wait until tomorrow, no pressure, okay?"

"Thanks, Gil. Let me see what LuAnn wants to do and I'll get back to you. Thank you for all you've done to make us comfortable, we appreciate it."

Gil laughed. He seemed like a jovial man. "It's the least I can do for my new bike designer and his girl."

Chase opened his mouth to say he hadn't accepted yet, but Gil's laugh on the other end stopped him.

"Thank you. Maybe we'll see you in a bit."

"Sounds good, Chase."

The line went dead before another word could be said and he thought it might be fun to see what the crowd here is like.

Check in was a breeze; Gil was right, he had it all set up. Their room was phenomenal, the service top notch and it was hard not to be taken in by this five- star treatment.

LuAnn walked out of the bathroom and up to him. Her arms slid around his waist and she hugged him close. "This is amazing, but not as amazing as you."

He pulled her closer, hugged her to him and enjoyed the feel of her body close to his.

"Want to go to a pig roast?"

45

Dressed in jeans and a Harley shirt, a cute one with rhinestones and cutouts, LuAnn was eager to see how this group partied. You could tell a lot about a dealership by how its chapters partied. If they were mean and rowdy it said as much about the owner of the dealership as those who loved to have fun without being sassy and disrespectful. That would give them a wealth of information and it was probably better that they saw this first before meeting formally tomorrow.

Chase took her hand as they walked across the parking lot toward the gates behind the shop where the party was in full celebratory mode. The music grew louder the closer they got, the laughter did as well. And that's what struck her, there was so much laughter.

A woman stopped them at the gates. "Are you members here, handsome?" She asked Chase.

He smiled at her and she dang near dropped to the ground. Yes, he was that impressive. "No, ma'am, we're guests of Gil's."

It took the woman a moment to recover, but she finally turned to a man leaning against the wall a few feet away. "Jack, where's Gil?"

"I'll get him." Jack stood up straight, glanced over at them, grinned, then walked into the crowd gathered around a bar, which looked to be constructed just for this purpose.

The woman turned to them and asked, "What's your name?"

Grinning Chase pulled up their hands, which were still clasped together, kissed her knuckles then replied, "This beautiful woman is LuAnn. My name is Chase."

"Chase," she muttered. LuAnn wondered if she were going to start drooling.

"Chase, so glad to see you." A tall man, clearly in his fifties, muscular for a man his age, boomed as he walked toward them. His white hair was cropped short and his white beard neatly trimmed made him look like muscular Santa. Though he'd need a bit of padding around the middle.

"Gil, it's great to finally meet you in person."

They shook hands and Gil pulled Chase in for a quick hug, then stepped back and looked directly into her eyes. "And this little blue-eyed beauty must be LuAnn. Nice to meet you, LuAnn."

He held his hand out and she shook it and smiled her biggest smile. "It's nice to meet you, too, Gil."

Gil turned toward the party and the bar he'd just come from and called over his shoulder. "Come on and meet the crew."

He squeezed her hand and tugged her along with him, and she tried to look where they were going but there was so much to see. The back lot looked like an old western town and some folks were dressed up in western wear. There were gals walking around delivering drinks in Daisy Dukes, cowgirl boots, red and white checked shirts and cowboy hats. They weren't taking any money, just delivering the drinks.

Gil stopped at a small group at the end of the bar. "Boys, this is Chase, who I hope will be our new designer, and his woman, LuAnn. Remember I showed you the white bike he built last year? Chase this is Buddy, Lane and Cowboy."

Each of the men took turns shaking hands, offering welcomes and asking what they wanted to drink. She wasn't sure who was who, but figured if she needed to know later, she'd figure it out. They were each given a beer and Gil turned to them, and said, "Let's go and I'll introduce you to some of the other members of our staff."

Nodding to the men at the bar, they followed Gil to another group of people sitting at a table in front of a "Sundries" storefront. They were once again introduced and continued to meet even more of the folks. Basically, what she got out of this was Gil had a large staff and a huge payroll. But everyone was polite and pleasant, and she felt oddly relaxed and, dare she say it, at home.

It felt like they'd met a hundred people before long and, unfortunately, Gil saw her yawn at one point which caused her cheeks to burn bright.

"I'm so sorry. Please know that I am not bored. I guess I'm just a bit jet lagged."

Gil laughed and that confirmed it, he absolutely was Santa Claus.

Chase looked at her and smiled. "I'm happy to go back to the hotel if you are. I'm feeling a bit overwhelmed myself."

"I don't want your time here to be anything less than you want it to be."

He leaned down and kissed her, and a couple guys whistled from her left. Chase looked over at them and smiled, then pecked her lips again.

"Let's say goodbye, we'll be back here tomorrow anyway."

"Okay."

"Gil, we're going to say good night, we were up before dawn and it has been quite the day."

"Completely understand, Chase. See you both at nine tomorrow. I'll show you out through the side gate, so you don't have to talk to everyone on your way out. Easier that way or you'll get sucked into several more beers."

Gil led them through a wooden storefront that said, "Bath 5 cents". Just through that doorway was a gate he had to enter a code to open, then he stepped out and held the gate for them. Stepping through the gate she saw they were right in front of where they'd parked. They'd essentially gone in a complete circle though it sure didn't feel like it.

Gil turned and shook Chase's hand. "Thanks for coming Chase, I look forward to our meeting tomorrow." He turned to her and shook her hand. "LuAnn, it was surely a pleasure to see such a pretty young lady come through our doors."

Her cheeks burned. "It seems as though you have plenty of pretty women here, Gil."

He chuckled, "Darlin, most of them are local waitresses hired for this event."

Deep in her stomach, she felt better that Chase wouldn't be working with those gorgeous women on a day-to-day basis. She would have to be blind not to see the way women looked at him. He was simply gorgeous. It still boggled her mind that she didn't see it before. Then again, he looked different now. His hair was rich, and full and long, which brought out the brown of his eyes, while before she went to prison, his hair had been long, it had also been sort of stringy and bleached blond from the sun. He held himself taller now, more confident and it was sexy on him. All of it.

46

Driving back to the hotel he enjoyed seeing the town as the sun set. "Do you mind if I detour through town?"

"No, not at all, I'd love to see it."

Chase turned left at the stop light and they drove down what looked to be an older part of Main Street. It was picturesque as the orange sun set behind the mountains beyond the buildings.

"It's beautiful," LuAnn said as she watched the city.

"It certainly is."

They drove out of this part of town and just a couple miles away they drove past a lake. The water was smooth as glass, the orange waning lights of the sun shone brightly on the water which now looked like a piece of glass.

He heard LuAnn mutter, "Wow," And his heart filled. It was breathtaking here.

As they drove around the lake he saw the homes nestled along the shore; they were spaced far enough apart that they allowed each homeowner some privacy. He turned down the road that looked to follow the lake and they stared out the windows at the spectacular homes on the lake.

As they rounded the bend in the road, he saw the prettiest home. It was nestled in the crook of the road on what looked to be an inlet. It wasn't the expensive looking stone or brick of the other homes; it was a more western design with its wooden siding and the large stone so common out here. He stopped in front of it and stared at the home. It was moderately landscaped, but you could see slightly toward the lakeside of the home that the landscaping was more extensive. A long dock led out to the lake and there was a bench at the end of the dock. It looked as if a man was out there fishing.

"Are you interested in this house, Chase?"

He looked into LuAnn's eyes, which seemed confused. She tilted her head to the side, and he smiled.

"I guess for some reason it speaks to me. Is that stupid?"

She smiled. "No."

She looked down at her phone and typed something into it. He continued looking at the stone steps, the shrubs, the boat on wooden stands alongside the house to the left. Then he saw it. It was for sale.

LuAnn turned her phone toward him. She'd looked it up by address and showed him the price. With his new salary, he could afford it. His heart raced at the thought. He could sell his Green Bay home and they could move out here and live on a lake. It would be pure magic. A place to come home to after a day of designing and dealing. They could sit on the dock in the evenings and have a beer or two. He'd learn how to fish. His mind raced with all the possibilities of what could be.

He finally looked at LuAnn, who had turned her head to stare at the house.

"What do you think, do you want to see it?"

Her head swiveled back to him; her lips curved just slightly. "Don't you think we should make sure you'll like your job here? I mean, I'd hate to fall in love with this house only to have you not really like what you'll see at the shop tomorrow."

He put the Jeep in park and twisted in his seat facing her. "What is your gut impression of what you saw tonight? Don't think about it, just say it."

"Everyone seemed nice. Like they all got along. Happy."

"Yes, that was my impression too. What else?"

"They weren't sure we were coming though they could have expected it. But, it didn't seem rehearsed or over the top."

"Yes." His hand wrapped around the back of his nape, and he rubbed his neck.

"Does it seem too good to be true?"

"I don't know." She shrugged and swiveled her head from side to side.

"Tell me what's bugging you. I need to know."

"It's stupid."

"Hey." He waited until she looked up at him. His fingers tucked under her chin and he stared into her eyes, which honestly wasn't a hardship. "I need to know."

She swallowed what looked to be a lump in her throat. "The women are gorgeous. I saw..." She stopped and swallowed. "I saw the way they looked at you. That's a lot of temptation to have to wade through every day."

He leaned down and kissed her lips. Tender. Soft. Gentle.

"Don't you notice how the men look at you?"

Her brows furrowed. "Honestly, Lu, you don't see it? They look into your gorgeous eyes, then their eyes travel to your voluptuous breasts, and as you walk away, they are all looking at your fantastic ass. I can't believe you don't see it."

Her fingers twisted in her lap and she shook her head. "I'm too busy worrying about which of the women I'm going to have to beat off with a stick for you."

He chuckled. "I'll tell you which ones. None of them. Sweetheart, I've waited three years for you. More if you count the years prior that I was so fucking in love with you and all you could see was Dog. I only want you."

A lone tear slid down her right cheek and he wiped it away with the back of his fingers. Kissing her lips once more he deepened his kiss to show her he meant what he said. And he did, he only wanted her. If he'd been enticed at all while she was in prison it was by Olivia, and even then he wasn't all that interested or he would have made time for her.

He rubbed his nose gently against hers then sat back. Looking over her shoulder at the house once more, he said, "Should we call and set a time while we're here to see the inside?"

"I can arrange that."

She tapped out an email to the agent listed on the internet listing and he continued around the lake looking at the homes, but not seeing anything he liked better than the one they'd stopped in front of.

Hopefully, there wouldn't be any downside shown to him tomorrow.

She sat nervously with Chase in Gil's office as he finished a telephone call. He genuinely seemed like a good boss. No one was edgy or cold around him and she'd watched when they first walked into the store to see how the employees treated each other. Her only experience in a bike shop was at Rolling Thunder, but one thing she knew for sure, Dog insisted problems be dealt with immediately, so they didn't fester, and he was kind to everyone. Look how he'd treated her even when she was being a bitch to Joci. That thought left her stomach sour, so she turned her head and looked at the pictures on the wall and tried to focus on something else.

"Okay, I'm sorry I had to take that. We're working on a new supplier for some of our clothing and I needed to get that taken care of."

Chase leaned forward, elbows on his knees, "It's just fine. It gives me a chance to see how you operate."

Gil laughed and she thought again about Santa. A handsome Santa. "That's good. From what I understand Dog treats all of his employees very well, so I get you don't want to leave a good place only to jump into a bad one. No worries at all and when you and I are finished talking, you are welcome to walk around and chat with any of the employees. I promise I didn't tell them to lie to you."

"Good to know." Chase chuckled.

"So, should we go and see the design shop?"

Gil stood and so did she and Chase. As Gil walked to the door, he chuckled. "You're gonna love this."

Exiting his office, they walked two offices down the hall to a nice office with two desks in it. There was a large computer screen and two smaller ones attached to the same computer.

"From what the salesperson told me, you'd need multiple screens to fully create, show parts lists, different color schemes and the like, so we bought the whole caboodle. No one here knows how to use this system, so I'd have the company come on out and give you training on it if needed."

Chase walked to the computer, shook the mouse and the screens lit up. He clicked a few times and was able to get a test bike up. He turned to them and said, "This is how you begin. I've not used this software before, but a little training and it'll be a cake walk."

She was so proud of him. Not only was he smokin' hot, but he was smart, too, and creative. Hell, he was the whole damned package.

She walked around the office while Chase and Gil chatted about budgets and bikes. Chase pulled out his note pad and showed Gil some of his designs and she listened as Gil praised them and told him how excited he'd be to showcase a Chase Matthews Design. They talked about timeframes for building and Chase would have one dedicated employee of his choosing to help him build and other miscellaneous things. There was a large window on one side of the office that looked out into a shop area and Gil told Chase that's where he'd build and bring his bikes to life.

"Let's go look," Gil said and they followed him out to the shop.

She stood back as Gil showed Chase around and gave him information about the equipment, the tools, and where the sheet metal was stored, and on and on. She watched Chase's face as it lit brighter and brighter as the meeting wore on. She knew he was sold. They were likely moving to Durango and she felt excited and then again, a little sad to leave behind all she knew especially Forget Me Nots and the wonderful people there who gave her a chance and taught her so much. But it was the right decision and a fresh start sounded absolutely wonderful.

Her phone chimed and she pulled it up to see an email reply from the realtor for the house. She had time this afternoon, did they?

She looked over at Chase as he smiled at Gil and they discussed something more. He was animated and, well, happy. Then it occurred to her that she hadn't seen him truly happy like this for a long-damned time. He needed the fresh start, too.

Typing out a response to the realtor, "Yes. How about 2:00?"

She sent the email and received a reply almost instantly. "Perfect. See you at the house."

She tucked her phone into her back pocket and Chase looked over at her. She winked and he smiled one of his biggest smiles and damnit if her panties didn't dampen.

Gil and Chase walked toward her, and Gil said, "LuAnn, I surely don't mean to ignore you, if you have questions, you should just blurt them out."

She giggled. "I'm fine, it's interesting."

Gil laughed. "I doubt it but it sure is nice of you to say." He began walking toward the door to the store. "Let's go and see the rest of the store."

They left the garage area and walked to the store and she couldn't believe the array of clothing, bike parts, signs, glasses and other bike related memorabilia he had stocked out there. She walked around and looked at the items and Gil came up beside her and said, "I'll find a place for you here if you want to work at Chief's, LuAnn. Anything to keep our designer happy."

She smiled and turned to face Gil. "That's very kind of you, but I'd prefer to find a job outside of here. Please don't take offense, but I'm a florist and would like to stay in that field if possible."

"Well, I'll be danged. A florist. That's fantastic. I completely understand."

They visited a while longer, and Chase asked Gil numerous questions as they meandered around the store. They met many of the employees and a few customers and Gil had to excuse himself for a telephone call.

Chase walked up to her and put his arm around her. "Do you have questions?"

She looked up into his eyes. "Not a one. How about you?"

"Yes. How do you feel about moving to Durango?"

48

She smiled at him and looked deep into his eyes. "Is this what you want? Will you be happy here?"

"I swear to God, LuAnn, I will be so fucking happy here. This is like a dream come true. On top of designing, did you hear what he'll pay me? Double my salary at Rolling Thunder plus a commission on each bike sold. Plus, state of the art equipment and tools. It's like I've fallen into the place of my dreams."

Her right hand cupped the left side of his face and smoothed over his cheek and jaw.

"As long as I'm with you, I'll be happy anywhere and that's no lie."

He gazed deep into her eyes for a long time; deciding she wasn't lying. He pulled her into his arms and hugged her so tight she actually gasped for air.

"My God, I love you true."

"I love you true, too, Chase."

When her arms tightened around him his heart felt like it would explode.

"Also, we can look at the house at 2:00 today."

He spun her around, lifting her feet off the floor and whispered in her ear. "It's meant to be. All of this is meant to be."

Gil's laugh could be heard as he walked up behind him. Setting LuAnn's feet on the floor, he turned to face Gil.

"Is this what I think it is?" Gil asked.

"It is. I accept."

Gil's hand reached out quickly and grabbed his in a firm handshake. "I can't tell you how happy this makes me. I've had my eye on you for a longtime, young man."

"Thanks, Gil." He looked down at LuAnn. "We're very excited about this opportunity."

Gil reached forward to shake LuAnn's hand, but as their hands clasped, he pulled her in for a hug.

"We have to make it official. You're part of the family now."

LuAnn laughed, and Gil said, "Why don't we go and celebrate?"

LuAnn answered first, "Well, we have a house to go and look at soon. Can we celebrate later?"

Gil's laugh was loud, deep, and genuine. "A house you say. Where pray tell is this house?"

Chase's excitement was bursting through. "Out on Waverly Lake"

"Oh, well, I think I know which house that is and let me tell you, it needs a bit of work. The old man who owns it hasn't been well for a number of years now and he's let things go. But, it's a gorgeous piece of property and the house has potential just go in knowing that and you'll be fine."

He shook Gil's hand. It was nice to have someone who knew the area and could offer some opinions. Turning to LuAnn, he said, "Babe, pull it up on your phone again."

He watched as her thin nimble fingers tapped on her

phone. She turned her phone to him, and he turned it to Gil.

"What do you think about the asking price? We're not familiar with the area."

"I'll tell you what, Chase. You offer him $20,000 less than he's asking, and I'd bet my right nut he'll take it."

"That will give us wiggle room to fix what needs to be fixed then. Thanks, Gil."

"You bet. You two have a great afternoon. How about we celebrate later in the week? I've got meetings all day tomorrow and Wednesday. Thursday I'm free. Why don't we plan on seeing some of the finer points of the area? At least unless you've seen them already."

Glancing at LuAnn, he saw her smile and he nodded to Gil. "Sounds like a plan."

Gil waved and headed toward his office and Chase took LuAnn's hand and headed toward the door. As they left the dealership, his heart was happy, and he felt...free. For the first time in a long time, he felt free. This puzzled him because he didn't really remember not feeling free before.

He opened the passenger door and waited for LuAnn to climb inside. Her slender legs encased in nicely fitting denim jeans always caught his attention. Her biker style boots peeked under the leg of her jeans and he thought that was the sexist way she could dress. Well, that was likely a stupid statement because for the weddings this weekend she looked fucking hot in her blue dress and heels. But, for some reason, that wasn't them. Not daily anyway. They were jeans and t-shirts kind of people and that was one of the things he really liked about LuAnn. She didn't fuss about pretty clothes or needing new shoes to go with every outfit. The boots she was wearing now were actually many years old.

Leaning in he gave her a kiss, closed her door and

walked around the back of the Jeep taking another glance at the dealership.

He saw two of the shop guys sitting at a picnic table and drove up to where they sat. He stopped the Jeep and called their names, one was Buddy, they'd met him last night.

"Hey, Buddy. Mind if I ask you a few questions?"

"Not at all."

Chase looked at LuAnn. "I'll be right back."

She smiled at him. "Okay."

He hopped from the Jeep, walked to the picnic table, and sat down. Shaking first Buddy's hand, then after he was introduced to the second man, Tank, he shook his.

"Can you give it to me straight? How is Gil to work for?"

Buddy started first. "I've been here seventeen years. Gil is honest to God one of the nicest men I know. He expects a good day's work, but he pays us well and treats us good. Not many like that around."

Tank nodded. "I'll second that. I've only been here three years, but I'll tell you I worked for some pricks before. Yelling. Screaming. Swearing. Bullshit answers to questions. Shitty shop conditions. This is like heaven compared to that shit."

Nodding, Chase processed these answers but didn't say anything else. Usually, if you let folks talk, you heard great information.

Tank chuckled. "Last year we had an issue. Someone was stealing from the store. Gil was trying to figure out why the books were so off and there was a week there where he was very quiet. I think he wasn't sure who was stealing from him, and he was feeling betrayed. Which he was. But soon enough his security cameras caught the culprit. Some shop rat he'd hired within the year was taking shit at the end of his shifts."

"Oh, that's right. That son-of-a-bitch got busted and is now in jail for theft for a couple of years. Dumbass." Buddy mused shaking his head.

"Thanks, you guys, just checking it all out."

"Welcome aboard, Chase, you'll like it here for certain." Buddy said.

"Thanks, guys. It just helps to chat with everyone to make sure. I've got a good boss now and I hate to leave there only to hate it here."

Tank laughed. "You won't hate it here. If you do, there's something wrong with you."

49

Sitting in the driveway of the house on the lake, they both stared at the lake. It was perfect. The water rippled here and there, and the sun glinted on the ripples creating the most exhilarating effect. Then the water smoothed out and the sun's rays created different effects. It was hard to look away.

"While we're waiting for the realtor, let's go walk around," Chase said.

"Okay." She unbuckled her seatbelt and jumped from the Jeep excited to see the house. She'd thought about it during the night last night. She hadn't slept well, there was so much going on in her mind. They needed to make the right decision. It seemed as though it was a done deal. They were moving here, so it seemed natural that they'd need a house to live in. But buying one right away was a big step.

Chase walked around the front of the Jeep and took her hand. They walked in unison up the driveway, to the side of the house and into the backyard for the full view of

Waverly Lake. Houses dotted the shoreline here and there. Not so many that it was intrusive and, to be honest, the homes that showed were easily twice or more valuable than this one, but she didn't care. The bricks and stone on the other houses were cold and formal while this house, as she turned to look at it, was the warm and welcoming appearance she'd always liked in a home.

The weathered cedar shakes on the house, while they could use some cleaning and stain, spoke of a modesty that personified she and Chase. The full wraparound porch, while piled with old wooden boards, firewood and a couple mismatched chairs, would look spectacular with some matching rocking chairs and baskets of flowers strewn about. She'd have hanging baskets on all sides of the house and that in itself would change the overall look of the place.

A car door sounded, and she turned toward the lake and Chase. She watched him as he stared out at the lake, lost in some sort of trance. Giving his hand a squeeze, she smiled when he looked into her eyes.

"I think the realtor is here."

"Oh, I didn't hear a car."

Staring into his earnest, sexy eyes she whispered, "You've already fallen in love with this place."

It was hard to tell with the sunlight shining on them, but she could swear he blushed.

"Kind of."

"Hello, I'm Leslie Peyton, the realtor. You must be Chase and LuAnn."

Leslie reached forward and shook Chase's hand first, then hers. It didn't go unnoticed that her eyes slid up and down Chase's firm body before landing on his eyes. But, as Chase does, he looked over at her and smiled the most beautiful smile, you know, one of those panty melters, and she felt like the only woman alive on earth.

"We're anxious to see the inside," he then said.

Leslie pulled her phone from her purse, tapped a couple of times, then turned to walk to the front door. They dutifully followed her and as they climbed the last step to the porch, the bottom of the electronic lock box slid out revealing the key.

Pulling it from its hiding place, she quickly unlocked the door then stepped aside to let them in first. Chase leaned forward and twisted the knob on the door, then with his hand at the small of her back, he ushered her inside first, then stepped in before Leslie.

Her first impression was that it was darker than it should be and certainly some fresh paint and newer furnishings would make a difference. The old, worn, orange sofa, which looked to be a blast from the past, as in the 70s, made the place look much older than it was.

There was an olive-green recliner alongside the sofa which had seen better days. The curtains were worn and looked tattered in places. But, overall, the space was nice; it could be easily freshened up and the good thing was it didn't smell.

Turning to see the kitchen, which was open to the living room, the cabinets were an older wood, had been painted a few times as the chipped spots showed. But this last coat was a dark gray, which really darkened the room. She'd paint them white and the space would feel fresh and clean.

There was ample space in the cabinets and a view of the lake from above the sink, the sliding doors from the dining area and the windows in the hall were breathtaking. Imagine looking out of those windows at that view every day.

They completed their tour by looking at the bath and a half, the two bedrooms and the storage area alongside. There wasn't a basement in this house; the storage area served as that with a washer and dryer, the hot water heater, furnace, and circuit box. But it was somewhat neat, and they would keep this room so much neater, she had no doubt.

Walking back to the living area, Leslie asked, "What do you think?"

Chase looked at her again, his voice was soft when he asked, "Do you want to step outside and chat a minute?"

"Yes."

She didn't. It was clear he was in love with the place. She wasn't quite there yet, but she knew she would be. It was quiet here; they'd been there close to an hour and she'd barely heard another car. It was very different from where they lived in Green Bay. No one would just drop by here. Once they made friends though people would come out to the lake.

"We'll be back in a few minutes."

Then he took her hand and they exited by way of the patio doors. There were two old yellow-mesh lawn chairs facing the lake along the water's edge. He motioned to them and they walked toward them and took a seat. Chase inhaled a deep long breath, then exhaled slowly.

"I like it here, Lu. But, it won't mean anything to me if you aren't here with me. What do you think?"

He took both of her hands in his then, kissed the knuckles on each hand, then stared deeply into her eyes. Who was she kidding, she'd go back to prison if it made him happy, sort of.

"I can see the potential. We're both hard workers, we can make this place look amazing with some sweat and a lot of effort. Likely a little bit of money, too, but it won't be that bad."

His smile. God, it practically made her dizzy when it shined on her. "Thanks, Lu."

Then, he got down on one knee in front of her.

50

His heart raced in his chest to the point that it was almost painful. He'd been thinking about this for a long time now. Probably the last year. He'd even had the ring design in his head for that long. But, the first time they made love again, after she'd come home, he knew it then. The first time she'd told him she loved him, that sealed the deal. He had the ring made. It was unique. One of a kind. A Chase Matthews Design. All for her.

He fished that ring from his front pocket. He'd been carrying it around for the past few days, looking for the perfect moment. This was it.

Looking into her stunned eyes, her mouth fell open and as he took her left hand in his, he could feel her shaking.

"LuAnn Mason. You are without a doubt, the only woman who I've ever loved, and you'll be the only woman I ever will love. Your smile, your heart, your soul, I want to meld them with mine. I want us to start out here in Colorado, as a united pair, husband and wife, a couple that no man will put asunder. You and me - forever. Will you marry me?"

His eyes watched the tears that slid down her soft cheeks. His left hand held her shaking left hand and he waited what seemed to be an eternity. She opened her mouth and closed it, a soft sob emitted from her throat and she opened her mouth again.

"Chase..." A sob squeezed out again and she sucked in a deep breath and let it out in a whoosh. Then she tried again.

"Chase Matthews. I've made so many mistakes. I've shown bad judgment. I've been vengeful and hateful. I've been in prison for nearly killing Joci. I've hurt you so many times. For all of that, I am so sorry. But, what I know now that I was too blind to see before is that I love you. I'm so grateful that you still love me. Nothing would make me happier than starting our lives here as husband and wife. A united couple. Together in all things, including forging a new life. So, yes, Chase, I would be honored to marry you."

He slipped the beautiful ring on her finger, the sun catching every facet and creating the most spectacular color display she'd ever seen.

"Oh my God." She whispered as she looked at it. "Oh my God, it's spectacular."

"I designed it just for you. It's a flower, three carats, the center diamond a carat and a half, the petals of the flower the other carat and a half. It's been in my head for a long time. I wanted something that showed you I love you and enjoy your love of flowers. I want you to look at it every day and smile when you see it."

"Oh my God." Her arms flew around his neck and they fell backwards into the soft grass. Her lips found his and they covered his as their tongues danced together. He wrapped his arms around her and rolled them to the side, as he continued to kiss her lips, taste her mouth, feel her body pressed along his. This was the best feeling in the world.

When they needed air, her giggles reached his ears and he chuckled along with her.

"This is the happiest moment of my life, Chase."

"That's good, 'cause it's the happiest moment of mine, too."

He kissed her lips once more, then remembered the realtor they'd left inside.

"We should probably go and write an offer on this house and make it ours."

"You're right."

They sat up, LuAnn stood first, he was still a bit sore, but he managed, then hand in hand they walked back into the house through the patio doors. Leslie stood there as they walked in a smile on her face.

"I'll have a story to tell back at the office. I've never experienced that before." Her eyes landed on LuAnn. "I assume you said yes."

LuAnn giggled. "I did."

Leslie held out her hand, "Let's see it."

Showing her ring off, the smile on her face and the light in her eyes was something he hadn't seen in such a long time. She'd been weighed down by all the negativity back home and he was once again convinced this was the absolute right thing to do.

"Holy moly, that's gorgeous."

"Chase designed it. Thank you."

LuAnn's arm circled his waist, and immediately he wrapped his around her. It felt right. All of it.

He looked at Leslie, "So, we'd like to make an offer on this house."

She smiled for the first time since they'd first met her. "I assumed so after that performance. I have my laptop right here. Let's sit at the table and write it up for you."

It took about an hour to get the offer written, to discuss the finer points of the sale and what was included and what wasn't. They'd get an inspection and he'd have to get his house listed right away. He'd call Greg and see if he had a realtor in the congregation that could help him out and they'd then have to have the hardest talk of all. Dog. He wasn't looking forward to that conversation. His stomach tightened a bit as he thought about it, but in his heart, he knew this was what had to happen.

His phone rang at that time, he looked at the readout and saw none other than Dog on his phone.

Chase turned his phone to show her who was on the readout.

Leslie asked, "Do you need to take it?"

"No, I'll call him back later."

She sent them each a link to sign their offer from their phones. They signed and she announced, "I'll get this to the Seller and let you know what he says."

She stood, shook LuAnn's hand first, then Chase's. LuAnn smiled, apparently she got the hint. They followed her out the door. LuAnn turned to look at the lake one last time for today and her eyes landed on the two faded lawn chairs where she'd been proposed to. She wondered if she should have asked to keep those chairs as a keepsake.

Chase walked them to the Jeep, opened her door and kissed her before she stepped up into the passenger seat. She lay her palm on his left cheek, her thumb grazing over his lips, then she said, "I love you, Chase."

"I love you, too, Lu."

Smiling at her, he closed her door, walked around the front of the Jeep, glancing at her once, which sent a thrill all through her body, then he climbed in the Jeep. Instead of starting it up right away, he sat staring at the lake, the slice of it they could see from this vantage point. It was peaceful.

With a heavy sigh, Chase started the Jeep and backed them out of the driveway. Instead of turning toward the exit, he turned them right and down the round that circled the lake. As they got to the other side, he stopped the Jeep and they peered through the trees to see their house from this view. It looked a bit run down now, but they'd have it looking sharp, yet warm and cozy in no time. Until she found a job, she'd have the time to handle getting all the pots planted and painting to make it a nice home for Chase.

"I hate waiting," he said as he stared across the lake.

She chuckled. "I do, too."

He looked at the clock on the dashboard and announced the time. "It's 3:30 p.m. The courthouse is likely open until 4:30, should we see what we have to do to get a marriage license?"

Surprised was the first word that came to mind. "You mean you want to get married right away?"

"Yeah, Lu. How else are we going to start our life here as a united couple?"

"Oh, wow. Okay, I wasn't sure you meant right away." She looked at him and she saw sincerity in those gorgeous dark brown eyes.

"Okay, let's go find out."

Life with Chase would always be the best adventure of that she was certain.

Pulling up the courthouse on her phone, she searched the laws about marriage licenses and found it.

"It says here, we both must be present, there is a $30 application fee and there is no waiting period. So, we could get married right away and you have to get married at least within 35 days from the date of issue."

She looked down at her clothing. Jeans and a Harley t-shirt. It was cute, but she'd at least prefer to look a bit dressier for their wedding. He chuckled.

"I see what you're thinking. Tell you what, why don't you call and see if we can get a time for tomorrow. We'll go dressed a bit better and have our day then. For tonight, we'll celebrate the engagement, tomorrow the wedding."

"That sounds like a wonderful idea."

She searched for the phone number, found it and tapped call. As the phone rang on the other end she watched the road and hoped this would soon be close to their new home.

"La Plata County Courthouse."

"Hi, I'd like to schedule a wedding for tomorrow if possible."

"Sure." She could hear clicking on the other end of the phone as the woman no doubt looked through an online calendar.

"We'd have 10:00 a.m. Or 3:00 p.m. Which do you prefer?"

Chase looked over at her and mouthed, "10:00 a.m."

Giggling, she responded, "10:00 a.m., please."

She answered the woman's questions. Their names, etc. And reminded them to get there at least 45 minutes earlier to get their license squared away.

Hanging up she looked over at Chase, and said, "You'll be my husband just after 10:00 a.m. tomorrow. No more time for regrets."

He laughed. "No regrets, babe."

"Good." She smiled as she looked down at her ring. The sun still shined brightly in the sky, but it wasn't nearly as beautiful as her ring.

"Oh no. We have to get rings. I don't have a ring for you. Do we have time to do that?"

His smile was beautiful. Infectious. "Yes, of course, there must be a jewelry store in town, look it up."

Quickly typing in jewelry stores she scrolled through the chain stores, thinking maybe a local jeweler would be best. Finding two, she tapped the directions to the first one and her GPS began telling them which way to go. It said only 5.3 miles, so they'd be there soon.

Excitement raced through her body as she thought about all that had happened today. Funny how life could change so much in one day. She'd thought about marriage, but honestly wasn't sure Chase was there with her yet. To hear he'd been thinking about this for some time was amazing. Also, a bit head spinning. Who knew he loved her so much? She would have been afraid to hope for that.

He slowed and pulled to the curb in front of a beautiful jewelry store. The outside had polished wooden trim around the exterior. Its window sparkled like the diamonds displayed inside it and the red carpet that led them to the door was a very posh touch.

Entering they were greeted by a nice, younger man wearing a very smart suit in dark blue and a crisp white shirt with a matching blue tie.

"Welcome to Bernstein Jewelers. Is there anything, in particular, I can help you with?"

Taking the lead this time, she said, "We need wedding bands."

Chase corrected her. "Actually, just one wedding band, for me. I've got hers already."

Her brows furrowed as she looked up at him. "You do?"

"Yes, Lu, it's a set."

"Oh." She swallowed. "Wow."

He chuckled and ushered her further into the store as

the young clerk walked to a glass case filled with wedding bands.

"What are you thinking? Silver? Gold? Tungsten?"

Chase responded without a thought. "Tungsten."

He wrapped his right arm around her shoulders, and she shook her head. He had really given this a lot of thought. She felt stupid that she hadn't. But, she was honestly afraid to get that confident about it. The last thing she needed was to have her heart broken.

52

Chase woke up hearing the shower running. A quick glance at the empty bed beside him confirmed that LuAnn was already up and very excited to get ready. He chuckled as he glanced at his phone for the time and realized it was already 8:00 a.m. It wasn't all that early. They'd done a fair amount of celebrating last night. A bottle of champagne in the room, along with strawberries dipped in chocolate, compliments of the hotel upon hearing their great news. Then, they'd made love just like they liked it. Long, slow and oh so good.

Touching her made his skin feel better. Kissing her made his lips feel as though they'd been made to kiss her lips. Sliding into her warmth, well, that made him feel like she was put on this earth to be his. And, that was what he was going to do today. Make it legal.

Tossing the covers back, he walked to the bathroom, his erection already growing as he thought about how she felt last night.

As he opened the door, his phone rang, and he let out a long sad sigh. Shit.

Stalking back to the bedside table he saw the caller's name. Dog.

He rolled his head back and forth, sat down on the bed, with his back to the headboard, clutched the covers and pulled them over his now softening erection and answered the phone.

"Morning."

"Good morning, Chase. I'm sorry to bother you but I wanted the chance to talk to you. Is this a good time?"

"I have a few minutes, but I have an appointment at 9:15 I have to be on time for."

"Okay. So, listen, I feel bad about how things went down at the weddings. I know I've apologized, but I could tell you were still pissed at me when you left, and I don't blame you. I am so sorry, Chase. I shouldn't have accused LuAnn of trying to harm Maddie and Dakota."

His heartbeat sped up and he was getting mad all over again. "Shouldn't you be telling this to LuAnn?"

Silence on the other end had him wondering if their call had dropped. "Dog?"

"Yes. I should. And, I will. But I wanted to talk to you first. To apologize to you first. You're like a son to me Chase and I feel bad that I let you down."

LuAnn walked out of the bathroom, wrapped in a clean white towel, her long toned legs stretched in one direction, her collarbone and neck in the other. The outline of her voluptuous breasts stretched the towel in the most delicious way, and he started getting hard again.

"Thanks for calling and letting me know. I'm disappointed, but you know how I feel. About both of you."

"I do know how you feel. Joci's been the only mature and forgiving one about what LuAnn did. None of us even knew how she felt. You were there. You heard her say that being mad was exhausting. Afterward she told me she's felt that way for a long time. She's been talking to me about my vitriolic behavior toward LuAnn and how it's hurt my relationship with you, especially since LuAnn came home. She told me I would regret it if I didn't get past bitterness." He paused, then continued, "When LuAnn saved Maddie's life Joci and I were so grateful although it may not have seemed that way. I know Joci trusts her. When I told LuAnn that I would try to stop always expecting the worst of her I meant it. I'm trying.

I know it's been a long time since this happened, and you may not understand how hard it is for me to come around. Imagine if a girl you knew and helped, nearly killed LuAnn and a baby she was carrying. How would you feel, even if you were blessed to have them live, about the person who did it whatever her intent?

I had no intention of telling you all of this now, but I want you to know that I am trying. I'll call LuAnn and apologize to her."

Chase was stunned and his anger was replaced by a mixed bag of feelings, the most prevalent, warmth.

"Why don't you give it a few hours?"

"I'll call her this afternoon."

"Okay. Thanks."

"Bye, Chase."

Hitting the 'end call' icon, Chase set his phone on the bedside table and pulled the covers away from his rock-hard cock.

LuAnn smiled as she looked at his erection. Slowly walking toward him, she untied the towel and let it fall to the floor. There she was in all her naked beauty. Her slender body had always been so enticing but she was even more slender now, toned from working outside in the dirt, shoveling and lifting heavy plants and pots. Her narrow waist expanded in both directions, into curvy hips and her voluminous breasts. She'd always had the best tits ever. Her perfectly pink round nipples puckered now as the cooler air touched her and hopefully her excitement grew.

She was fluid in her movements as she climbed up his body, her breasts swaying with each movement. Her eyes, first on his, then on his cock, she licked her lips then slid her mouth over his penis and he groaned. Life was so fucking good.

Not sure which was better, watching her head bob or watching her lips stretched over his cock as they slid up and down. The warmth of her mouth coupled with the sucking had his balls tightening up in record time. He pulled on her shoulders to bring her up to him, so he didn't come too fast, but she sucked harder and he dropped his head back against the headboard knowing it was futile. She was going to suck him off in record time and then marry his ass. What a fantastic way to start the day.

She increased her speed and then the sucking and he groaned out loud as his orgasm slammed into him, first the pain of his balls so tight into his body then the pleasure as the release hit. He could feel himself spurt a few times, but she sucked down every drop.

His heart hammered in his chest as she licked him one last time, his eyes were closed, and he enjoyed her gentleness now where before she'd been eager to get him off.

She kissed her way up his torso, sucked in each nipple until they puckered, then kissed his lips.

"I love you, Chase Matthews, but we're getting married in about 70 minutes."

He laughed. "Damn it, Lu, you want me to walk around when my legs are like jello now?"

She laughed, and crawled off the bed, heading for the bathroom once again. He allowed himself a bit of time to regain all of his senses, then he followed her into the bathroom, and hopped in the shower while she brushed her teeth.

Damn vixen.

But, today was the first day of the beginning of their lives as husband and wife. Tonight, he'd make sure she had no regrets.

53

They walked into the Judge's chambers, which was beautifully appointed. The floor to ceiling wooden walls with the golden seal of the State of Colorado, and little else was rich and warm, but a bit austere for a wedding. Maybe they could have a vow renewal in a few years and make it more of something they'd want for their celebration. They'd have made friends here by then, it would be fantastic. He thought about his conversation and tried pushing it away.

Judge Webster walked in through another door that was part of the wall. It surprised her to see it open. The judge then smiled at them.

"That goes to the courtroom."

She was wearing her robe smartly with nothing of her clothing showing except her navy pant legs from under her robe. A string of pearls draped at her neck was the only adornment she wore. No earrings, no bracelets, no rings. Her light hair was pulled back into a bun at the back of her head, but her bangs softened the severe hairstyle.

Relaxing a bit, LuAnn returned her smile. "Very clever."

"So, you two want to get married?"

Chase finally spoke. "Yes, ma'am. We're moving to Durango in a couple of weeks and we want to start our life here as husband and wife."

"How long have you known each other?"

Chase turned his head and met her eyes. He smiled, took her hand, kissed her knuckles and softly responded. "Five years."

Judge Webster smiled. "That's a much better answer than I usually get." She lay some papers on her desk then turned to face them.

"I can marry you here in my office, in the courtroom or across the street in the park."

LuAnn jumped to answer first, "In the park, please." Looking up at Chase, "It's alright, isn't it?"

"I think it's perfect."

Judge Webster opened a file drawer, pulled out a sheet of paper then looked up at them. "You have your marriage license with you?"

Chase pulled it from his back pocket and handed it to the judge. "Right here."

She opened the license, looked everything over, then looked at the sheet of paper she'd just pulled from her drawer.

"You can sign everything here then we can go to the park and you can say you're vows. It's very pretty this time of year."

The judge pointed to where they'd each sign their names, then she signed the license, picked it up and tucked it in a book. Standing she began walking toward the door they'd entered as she said, "Let's go get you officially married."

They walked downstairs and on their way out of the courthouse, Judge Webster stopped at the front desk and said something to the woman seated there. She nodded, then got up and left.

Chase held her hand all the way to the park, his fingers were firm but not in a nervous grip more as if he was worried she'd take off running. Crazy thinking, she'd never do that. More than ever, she knew he was the one, the one she'd spend her life with. Maybe they'd even have children. They hadn't talked about it, but as she looked into his eyes, having a child that was part him and part her would be amazing.

They entered the park grounds with its plush grass and colorful flowers. One end was a playground filled with laughter. Moms and dads sat on benches chatting and smiling at their children. The other end had a small pond and a covered patio or grandstand.

Judge Webster turned to them quickly, "That would be a beautiful scene for your vows, do you agree?"

Chase answered first. "Perfect."

When he looked down into her eyes she softly blurted out, "Do you want to have kids one day? We haven't talked about it."

Chase stopped following the judge and turned to face her. Taking both of her hands in his, he kissed her lips quickly then answered her. "I would love to be a father. Do you want kids?"

She was almost breathless. "Yes. Yours. I want your children."

He kissed her again, then said, "Let's get married so we can start on that."

She giggled, her heart lighter than it had ever been. They followed Judge Webster up the three steps to the domed grandstand. She stopped in the middle and turned to face them.

"Ready?"

"More than ready." Chase responded.

LuAnn smiled so big her cheeks hurt. "Ready."

Judge Webster looked past them, "Your witnesses are on their way."

LuAnn turned her head to look back and saw the lady from the front desk of the courthouse walking toward them with another lady. They stepped up onto the grandstand, both of them smiling.

Judge Webster opened her book and began reading the legal words that would make them husband and wife. She then asked, "Would you each like to say something?"

Chase looked into her eyes. "I would."

"As you say your vows, you can place your ring on her finger and vice versa."

She swallowed as he smiled at her. That perfect panty melting smile. He pulled her ring from the front pocket of his black dockers, ironed so they were smart but still casual. They'd opted for nice, but casual. She wore a blue sun dress she'd brought with her and a cute pair of white sandals.

"You make me feel whole. You make me feel powerful. You bring a light to my life that I honestly didn't know was missing. I look forward to each new day with you because you make me feel complete."

He pulled her engagement ring from her finger, then slid the gorgeous eternity band on her finger, the diamonds in it just as sparkly as her engagement ring, which he then placed on her finger on top of her wedding band. The pair together were as stunning as his eyes. As him. The whole of him was stunning.

She couldn't stop the tear that tracked down her cheek. It flowed out so fast and rolled down even faster. She gently sniffed, cleared her throat lightly then screwed up the courage to try and match those beautiful words.

"Chase." Her lips quivered and she paused, inhaled, and tried again. "You have taught me what patience is. You've taught me what guidance is. Mostly though, you've taught me what love is and I never want to be without your love. Ever. I will work hard every day to give you the same love you give me. Without fail. I love you."

She pulled his tungsten wedding band from her thumb and placed it on his finger. The darkness of the metal was so beautiful on his tanned masculine hand.

He leaned toward her, his eyes glistening with tears and lightly kissed her lips. "I love you more."

She giggled then Judge Webster completed their vows. "I now pronounce you husband and wife. This is where I say you may kiss the bride, but you already did that."

"I'm going to do it again." Chase teased. Then he did. His hands cupped her face and his lips claimed hers. It was gentle, but he fully kissed her lips, his tongue dipped in and explored her mouth, and she loved every damned minute of it.

He ended their kiss with a light kiss on the end of her nose. They turned to Judge Webster, who smiled at them sweetly, which made her look so much softer than she'd appeared previously.

"How about a few pictures for your memory book?"

Chase quickly pulled his phone from the pocket on his thigh, tapped a couple of times, the brand-new ring on his finger a sight to behold, then he handed his phone to the judge. She did a fantastic job of having them move and pose for certain pictures. They walked down close to the water, then in front of the grandstand, then on the steps. They'd have such nice pictures forever.

"Thank you for all of these pictures, Judge Webster." LuAnn said as they glanced through them.

She laughed. "My sister is a photographer, so I've

learned a few things over the years. I wish you both a happy life together."

LuAnn turned. She wasn't sure if it was proper, but she did it anyway. She walked up to the judge and wrapped her arms around her neck and gave her a hug. Whispering in her ear, "I will never forget you. Thank you."

She heard Judge Webster sniff and she smiled to herself. Softy.

54

Chase parked the Jeep in front of the restaurant. They were a few minutes early for their reservation. LuAnn's phone rang and his gut told him it was Dog.

She turned her phone to him, and he saw Jeremiah's number on the screen.

"I asked him to call you later today. He called me this morning."

"Why?"

"Answer it."

He saw her swallow a lump in her throat, then tap the answer icon, then the speaker.

"Hello."

"Hi, LuAnn, it's Jeremiah."

"Yes. I recognized your number."

"Of course." Dog inhaled deeply. "I wanted to apologize again to both of you for my behavior at the wedding. I had no right to accuse you of doing something wrong when what you did was sacrifice yourself for my daughter and granddaughter. For that, we are all eternally grateful."

"I didn't know whose children they were Jeremiah. I

saw two little girls in trouble and needed to help. If I would have known whose children they were, I would have done the same thing. You have every right to think the worst of me after my behavior in the past, and for that I apologize to you and Joci. It wasn't my intent to hurt her or Maddie let alone nearly kill them, but I did it. I own it. But you should also know, I've learned..."

She looked up at him, stared into his eyes and her lips smiled a soft smile. "I've learned so much. And while we can't predict the future, any of us, I know one thing for sure. I will never behave in that way again. I've grown. I'm grounded. I'm finally becoming the woman I want to be and can be proud of and I'll never be that other woman again."

The line was quiet again and Jeremiah cleared his throat. "Lance would be very proud of you LuAnn. Of that, I'm certain. As I told you, you I'm trying very hard to put the past behind me. Joci is helping me to see that I have to reach forgiveness for all of our sakes."

LuAnn nodded her head quickly, tears in her eyes. She tried saying something in return, but her voice was clogged with emotion, so he jumped in.

"Dog, I'm here with LuAnn and I was going to tell you this in person next week, but I may as well tell you now. This morning didn't seem the time to tell you either. I appreciate what you had to say, and you gave me some-thing to think about when you asked me how I'd feel if it was LuAnn." He reached forward and took LuAnn's left hand in his. "Anyway, LuAnn and I were married today and we're both ecstatic. And, we'll be moving to Durango, Colorado in the coming weeks. I've been offered a job out here at Chief's as head designer. I appreciate all you've done for me, including being the closest man I had as a father, but I honestly think this is better. I get to move forward in my career. LuAnn and I won't have to live with people snarling, jeering and basically holding her past against her and we get a clean, fresh start out here."

"Wow." Jeremiah cleared his throat, inhaled deeply and responded. "I'm very happy for both of you. I mean that with my whole heart. I'm sorry to lose you Chase, but you are one hell of a designer and you'll be a huge hit at Chief's. Gil is a great guy."

Chase swallowed and cleared his throat. "It all started with you, Dog. I will always love you and the guys. Always."

"Same here, Chase. Same here. Let's finalize things when you get back."

The line went dead, and he looked into LuAnn's watery blue eyes. But there wasn't sadness on her face. It was relief.

"I'm so happy to move out here and leave ugliness behind. I feel like we are really starting over now."

He leaned in and kissed her lips. "I'm glad to hear it. You deserve it and Dog needs to forgive you. I'm happy about what you said to Dog, too. Remember when you said that making amends was one of the things you needed to find peace?"

She nodded.

Well, I think you just did it and Greg will be glad for you. As for being happy to be moving out here, all I can say is me, too."

Turning to jump out of the Jeep, he walked around the front, cleared the emotion from his throat, straightened his shoulders and opened the passenger door. His phone rang and he halted LuAnn's progress, shrugged when he didn't recognize the number, she sat back and he answered the phone, speaker on.

"Chase Matthews."

"Hi, Chase this is Leslie Peyton. I have great news; the Seller has accepted your offer."

LuAnn's smile said it all. They were homeowners. Almost.

"That's fantastic. When can we close?"

"He's agreed to your closing date of 30 days. I'll email you the signed offer. Now it will be up to you to get your financing in order. I'll order the inspection. I just need some dates when you'll be available."

"Can I get back to you on that in a bit? LuAnn and I are just going in to celebrate our marriage."

"Congratulations. Wow, you folks move fast."

He laughed, "You have no idea."

He took LuAnn's hand, his wife's hand, and helped her from the Jeep. He kissed her knuckles. "We have a lot to celebrate Mrs. Matthews and a baby to make, so let's start this evening off shall we?"

55

Sliding the moving box onto the back of the moving truck, LuAnn turned to make another trip inside. Chase had been fortunate. With the help of one of Greg's parishioners, a realtor, he'd sold his house in a few days and the new owners were moving from another area and were eager to move quickly. He was right or lucky, but when it was meant to be it all worked out.

The sound of a motorcycle caught her attention. She stopped and turned to see Jeremiah and Joci stop at the curb of the house. She swallowed a large lump in her throat and willed her heart to beat normally. Sending up a silent prayer that this would be a good visit, she stood still and watched them as they walked across the lawn toward her.

Then, she remembered her conversation with Dog on her wedding day. It had been good. Chase had told her about his conversation with Dog before their wedding. It nearly blew her away to think that Joci was the first to forgive when she had felt so unworthy for so long. It was amazing that Joci was trying to get Dog to understand it was time to forgive her. She so hoped that he would, not for herself but for Chase. She knew that Chase and Dog loved each other and no matter how far away they were from each other, they'd want to keep in touch.

It suddenly occurred to her that she hadn't seen Joci since before the accident that sent Joci to the hospital and her to prison. She wanted to throw up. She wanted to run and find Chase, but she didn't want to appear the scared rabbit.

Joci greeted her first, "Hi, LuAnn. Marriage agrees with you, you're glowing."

LuAnn smiled; she didn't expect that.

"I'm actually sweating but thank you." Her eyes turned to Jeremiah. "It's nice to see you."

"It's nice to see you as well, LuAnn."

"Most of the furniture is in the truck, but there are some lawn chairs. Why don't you sit down, and I'll find Chase. I'm rather hot and thirsty. Would you like some lemonade?" she asked.

Joci answered, "Yes, that would be great."

The door behind her opened and she could feel Chase before he wrapped his arms around her shoulders.

Chase leaned forward and held his hand out to Jeremiah, who then pulled him in for a hug. She watched and her heart felt lighter seeing Chase and Dog hug.

"I told them I'd get some lemonade. Why don't you see if you can round up some chairs?"

When she returned they were sitting in the lawn chairs and Chase had found a small table. It was rather quiet while she filled the glasses. She sat in the empty chair between Chase and Joci. The couples sat close to their spouses.

Dog put his arm around Joci's shoulders, glanced down

into her very pretty gray eyes, then back to her. "We wanted to properly thank you for saving…

LuAnn said, "Wait. I have something to say first." She looked at Joci, and said, "I should have apologized to you before now. I am so sorry, Joci, for all I did to you since I first met you. I was young and foolish. I thought I loved Dog, but it was a schoolgirl infatuation which I realized in prison. I never meant to hurt you let alone try to kill you or Maddie. But my intent doesn't matter. I did it. And I am so ashamed and mortified by my behavior and so damned sorry. I don't expect anything from you, but I wanted you to know how I feel.

Joci's eyes filled with moisture, but she nodded and tried to smile.

Dog said, "As I started to say, we wanted to properly thank you for saving Maddie and Dakota.

She took a deep breath. "I thank you for that."

"I also wanted to tell you, LuAnn that I know I'll never forget what you did. But, you did your time, and as Joci keeps telling me life's too short to hold on to bitterness. So, I'm damn close to forgiving you. Give me a few more months." He smiled at LuAnn, and her eyes began to fill up, not for her but Chase. Joci's and Chase's eyes sparkled with the tears that threatened to fall.

"You work on getting there all the way, Dog" Chase said.

"Will do, Chase."

Dog said, "We also want to wish you well on your new journey in life. I simply couldn't stomach the ugly feelings left among all of us. I hope we've cleared the air or are really close if it weren't for some obstinate bastard." Everyone laughed easing the tensions about the serious things they'd been discussing.

"We're going to miss you so fucking much, Chase." Dog

stammered. His eyes were glistening with moisture and he swallowed a few times to calm himself.

"I'm going to miss all of you, too. This is a great opportunity for me." He turned and smiled at her. "For us."

"I have to agree with you. I called Gil and chewed him out for stealing you, then I thanked him for seeing the creativity in you. I know he'll treat you good. I've threatened to come and kick his ass if he doesn't."

That got them all laughing a bit and further lightened the mood. They all rose and headed toward the street.

Joci said, "Thank you for the lemonade and for working on the obstinate bastard to totally leaving the past behind." Everyone laughed again with Dog the loudest.

Chase stepped back and took her hand, kissed her knuckles, then looked back at Dog and Joci. "Honestly, if you're out in Colorado, please look us up. Our house is on Waverly Lake and it's so peaceful and beautiful out there you'll be impressed."

Joci smiled at Chase, then looked into her eyes. "We'll do that for a fact. We'd love to stay in touch." Dog nodded.

LuAnn found her voice. "We'd love that. Truly."

Another motorcycle pulled up and Greg hopped off his bike and walked toward them all.

Dog leaned forward and shook Chase's hand. "We'll take off, you'll be saying goodbye for days here. Take care you two and stay in touch." He nodded to her, Joci waved and they walked toward Greg, shook his hand then continued on and hopped on their motorcycle and left with another wave.

LuAnn inhaled deeply and released the tension held in her shoulders and back. They needed that.

Greg walked up and hugged Chase, then hugged her and she felt those darned tears spring to her eyes once again.

"Greg, I want to thank you for your counselling which helped me to find peace, which helped me to find myself."

Greg smiled, "All I did was help you find God. You did the rest."

She sniffed quietly, she should have stuck a tissue in her pocket, dang it.

Chase lightened the moment, "Come on into our mess, Greg."

She turned and entered the house, the men behind her and she quickly excused herself to grab a tissue in the bathroom.

When she walked back out to the kitchen, Greg and Chase both stood leaning against the counter waiting for her to come out, a beer in each of their hands.

"Lu, wait till you hear Greg's news."

Chase's smile was huge, his eyes dancing with delight.

Greg's cheeks tinted pink, and he cleared his throat. "Well, I mean, it's not news really, it's just, well, while you both were out in Colorado I met someone. We've seen each other a few times now and I really like her. So, we're, I guess…dating."

It was cute how embarrassed he was. Chase elbowed him lightly. "Tell her all of it."

Greg cleared his throat again. "Well, I'm dating Olivia, the owner of Lickety Split."

LuAnn's brows rose, a smile creased her face. She looked at Chase, who smiled back at her, then he winked.

"That's fantastic, Greg."

"Yes." His cheeks were now a bright red as were the tips of his ears.

Chase laughed. "When things are supposed to work out, they work out. Right, Lu?"

"Right." They shared a friendly laugh together.

They visited until the beer was gone, then Greg bid

each of them farewell, he had a date tonight, so he needed to be on his way.

They stood in the living room window, waving goodbye to their friend and confidant, and as his bike traveled out of sight Chase whispered. "That's a great match right there. I'm sorry I didn't think of it and set them up."

LuAnn laughed. "So, it's not enough you're gorgeous, built, talented, an amazing lover and my husband, now you want to be a matchmaker, too?"

He laughed and kissed her lips. Then he swatted her on the ass. "Quit dawdling Mrs. Matthews, we have to get our stuff to Durango before Monday."

"Yes, Mr. Matthews. New life. New house. New husband. New everything. We're moving on and I'm so excited to enjoy life with you."

KEEP READING to meet Levi and Sage - Heart Thief, Bluegrass Security Book One.

The weather had turned colder today; typical Nebraska weather—cool one day, warm the next. Pulling his stiff hands from his woolen coat pockets, Levi opened the door to the diner, and the warmth washed over him comingled with the delicious aromas of freshly baked biscuits and bacon frying in the kitchen. Nodding to the waitress, he found a seat in the booth in the corner—his favorite place. It was hard staying to yourself in this town. Everybody knew everyone and everything a person did; it was annoying. Although, in his line of work, it did come in handy to know some of the things going on. He tried to quietly keep tabs on everything within reason.

The waitress walked to his table, a skip in her step and a cheery smile. It was a bit too early in the day for that as far as he was concerned. She smiled brightly. "Mornin', Levi. The usual today?"

"Morning, Viv. Black coffee, two eggs over easy, an order of crispy bacon, and toast on the side."

She jotted something on her order form, then offered, "Yep, the usual. Be right back with your coffee."

She skipped away, and he took the opportunity to glance at her legs. She always wore shorts and tennis shoes when she worked. Her nail polish was always a different color and her red hair was always pulled up in some messy-looking do. She dressed a bit too young for her age —which he guessed to be mid-forties, maybe fifties—and she still maintained the vigor of youth. Whereas, he felt old beyond his forty-five years.

He frowned as he watched her briskly move behind the counter; she was a whirlwind of activity—smiling and waving—just a happy gal. He slightly shook his head as he glanced around the diner. The usual suspects were present this morning. Some of the older farmers gathered each morning to talk about crops, equipment, and to gossip about the goings-on in town. There was an elderly couple at the next booth, a couple of high school kids at one of the tables, a nice looking younger gal with long dark hair and a striking face at the table in the window, and a smattering of truck drivers at the counter. This week's gossip was especially juicy because the Halloween Festival was coming up next week and that's when the majority of the town's shenanigans happened. As soon as you added a haunted house, zombie shooting, a kissing booth, and a tarot reader to a small town, things that normally didn't occur began to happen.

It was sure as hell going to make his job harder this week. He hoped his new guy, Sage Reynolds, who should be arriving this afternoon—worked out. He'd started his security firm a couple of years ago, and he was finally starting to see some profit. Worried that profit would float away if this new guy and Chuck, his employee of about two weeks, didn't get trained to take on some of his work, Levi heaved out a heavy sigh.

"Here's your usual, Levi."

Continue reading about Levi and Sage, grab your copy here: https://books2read.com/Heart-Thief-Bluegrass-Security

Keep in touch and learn about new releases, sales, recipes, and other fun things by signing up for my newsletter - https://www.subscribepage.com/PJsReadersClub_copy

ALSO BY PJ FIALA

To see a list of all of my books with the blurbs go to: https://www.pjfiala.com/bibliography-pj-fiala/

You can find all of my books at https://pjfiala.com/books

Romantic Suspense

Rolling Thunder Series

Moving to Love, Book 1

Moving to Hope, Book 2

Moving to Forever, Book 3

Moving to Desire, Book 4

Moving to You, Book 5

Moving On, Book 6

Rolling Thunder Boxset 1, Books 1-3

Rolling Thunder Boxset 2, Books 4-6

Military Romantic Suspense

Second Chances Series

Designing Samantha's Love, Book 1

Securing Kiera's Love, Book 2

Second Chances Boxset - Duet

Bluegrass Security Series

Heart Thief, Book One

Finish Line, Book Two

Lethal Love, Book Three

Wrenched Fate, Book Four

Bluegrass Security Boxset, Books 1-3

Big 3 Security

Finding His Fire Book One

Finding His Mark Book Two

Finding His Jewel Book Three

Finding His Match Book Four

Big 3 Security Boxset, Books 1-3

GHOST

Defending Keirnan, GHOST Book One

Defending Sophie, GHOST Book Two

Defending Roxanne, GHOST Book Three

Defending Yvette, GHOST Book Four

Defending Bridget, GHOST Book Five

Defending Isabella, GHOST Book Six

RAPTOR

RAPTOR Rising - Prequel

Saving Shelby, RAPTOR Book One

Holding Hadleigh, RAPTOR Book Two

Craving Charlesia, RAPTOR Book Three

Promising Piper, RAPTOR Book Four

Missing Mia, RAPTOR Book Five

Believing Becca, RAPTOR Book Six

Keeping Kori, RAPTOR Book Seven

Healing Hope, RAPTOR Book Eight

Engaging Emersyn, RAPTOR Book Nine

GHOST Legacy (Next generation)

Finding Lara, Book One

Saving Elena, Book Two

Rescuing Kenna, Book Three

Protecting Everleigh, Book Four

Guarding Adelaide, Book Five

Shielding Maya, Book Six

ENJOY THIS BOOK? YOU CAN MAKE A BIG DIFFERENCE

Reviews are the most powerful tools in my arsenal when it comes to getting attention for my books. As much as I'd like to, I don't have the financial muscle of a New York publisher. I can't take out full page ads in the newspaper or put posters on the subway.

(Not yet, anyway.)

But I do have something much more powerful and effective than that, and it's something that those big publishers would die to get their hands on.

A committed and loyal bunch of readers.

Honest reviews of my books help bring them to the attention of other readers.

If you've enjoyed this book I would be so grateful to you if you could spend just five minutes leaving a review (it can be as short as you like) on the book's vendor page. You can jump right to the page of your choice by clicking below.

https://books2read.com/MovingOn-PJFiala

MEET PJ

Writing has been a desire my whole life. Once I found the courage to write, life changed for me in the most profound way. Bringing stories to readers that I'd enjoy reading and creating characters that are flawed, but lovable is such a joy.

When not writing, I'm with my family doing something fun. My husband, Gene, and I are bikers and enjoy riding to new locations, meeting new people and generally enjoying this fabulous country we live in.

I come from a family of veterans. My grandfather, father, brother, two sons, and one daughter-in-law are all veterans. Needless to say, I am proud to be an American and proud of the service my amazing family has given.

My online home is https://www.pjfiala.com.
You can connect with me on Facebook at https://www.facebook.com/PJFiala1,
and
Instagram at https://www.Instagram.com/PJFiala.
If you prefer to email, go ahead, I'll respond - pjfiala@pjfiala.com.